Feast Island

By Tamar Hela

Spirit Lake Series, Book One

EP|C

Epic Books Publishing

A boutique publishing company specializing in
Children's and Young Adult Literature
Visit us at: epicbookspublishing.com

Copyright © 2012 Tamar Hela
First Edition (1)

Cover Design by Cheryl Smith

Fonts: Bispo, Century, Journal, and Leander

Summary: Seven teenagers from Northern California are
assigned a seemingly innocent group project for their Freshman
English class. Little do they know, this project will take them on a
journey out of this world—literally. Cantelia, appears much like
Earth until the kids realize magic is as plentiful as the wildlife
surrounding them. A dark and evil ruler is enforcing a curse on the
tribes people of Sikuku Island—the same place where the kids have
been transported. Now, they must help the islanders break the curse
if they ever want to see their own planet again. Join Alex, Ben,
Heather, Daniel, Justin, Keira, and Geoffrey as they learn there is so
much more beyond their comfortable lives in Pollock Pines and its
legendary Spirit Lake.

[Fiction-Fantasy, Fiction-Young Adult, Fiction-
Paranormal]

ISBN-10: 0985454210
ISBN-13: 978-0-9854542-1-0

Book Dedications

This book is for Jessica B., who practically hounded me to finish it—in a good way. She has been the go-to person for me to throw ideas around and talk about my characters and world as if they all really exist. I get the best ideas from her, especially since she has the strangest fears. Ha! Thanks for being my number one fan, Jess.

This book is also for Justin, who encouraged me to start writing several years ago. Because of him, I took the writing bull by the horns and tamed it into this kitten of a book. JP, thanks for believing in me always—even when I've been a complete tool.

And finally, this book is for my grandfather, whom I affectionately called "Grumps". He always believed in me and told me I could do anything. Grandma says I was one of his favorites—well, he was one of mine. Miss you and love you lots, Grumps. Wish you were here to see my newest accomplishments.

Acknowledgements

Thanks to my family for love and support. Much love and gratitude to my beta readers. For my friends believing in and loving me—love you guys right back. Shout out to my current and former students who indulged me as I read snippets of this novel during our down times. My favorite local Starbucks (Almaden and Curtner store, yeah!) and Crema Coffee for keeping me comfy and well caffeinated on "writing weekends".

Former English teachers who gave me the best foundation in language and mechanics any girl could wish for. Lots and lots of love to my awesome publisher, R.W. More love to my editor, S.E. The BEST boss and mentor EVER who has always prompted me to follow my dreams and my heart. Wonderful co-workers who are so supportive and encouraging.

My writing group, from all of whom I've learned a great deal about the writing/publishing world—especially Brea, who gave me hope that I really could be a legitimate writer. Thanks my little sis, who has brought my book and characters to life through her amazing artistic skills. To all my "favorites"—you know who you are—especially Debbie. Holler to my book club ladies!

Oh yeah...and to Jesse: Hey boy, thanks for letting me call you "Cabana Boy" and for putting up with me. Now, where's my drink with the little umbrella?

Prologue: A Rumor

In the days where evil sat on the throne of the universe and dark magic shrouded Cantelia like a mist, people and other beings alike had long ago dismissed the belief that hope existed. Even remembering the days of light instead of darkness was too hopeful. Faith was as foreign a concept as the word itself.

As long as Diegen, the land's gruesome and lethal ruler, was pleased by the ceremonial sacrifices of flesh and the population remained stagnant, no one expected more than everyday events to happen. All stayed close to home, paid tribute to the one whose name sent chills down their spines, and didn't hold their breath while wondering if they would live to see the next day.

There was something that couldn't be ignored though—no matter how much *he* tried to shut it out. The Prophecy—the only ray of hope that someday soon, the evil days would cease their hold on the land and peace would return. Though it was absolutely forbidden and dangerous to speak of such a thing, hushed and secretive murmurs passed from neighbor to neighbor.

There were rumors of a sort of secret society—a

Brotherhood—that kept the prophecy alive and well. This covert group of brave and noble souls risked their lives just to meet and scrutinize every detail of the ancient scroll held sacred. They knew redemption and justice were near, which would both be products of the prophecy fulfilled. It was now only a matter of time until the young saviors appeared. They would be watching and waiting, ready to fight alongside their redeemers for their freedom, as soon as the time had come.

Feast Island

Chapter One: A Dangerous Love

Many years ago, there were four tribes on Sikuku Island, in the Land of Cantelia. Though they had their differences, all the tribes were at peace with one another, intermarrying and forming the bonds of friendship. The land area of the island itself was massive, but the population remained small. Therefore, Sikuku Island held no interest to Cantelia's evil and oppressive ruler, Lord Diegen. To him, the islanders were merely uninteresting chattel, illiterate and naïve at best.

On one fateful day, however, an incident occurred, ripping apart the blanket of peace that covered the island and its people. Though assumed to be petty, most have forgotten what exactly started the civil wars between the tribes. Again, Diegen couldn't have cared less. It was all the better to have the tribes fight and slowly commit their own genocide. Therefore, he turned a blind eye to their activities, allowing them to govern themselves with chaos, hate, and bloodshed.

Finally, the wars ceased. The tribes could not bear to lose any more of their own people. Each chief,

Wata, Kodu, Feldor, and Vang, sent their wise men to make some sort of treaty—not a peace treaty, but an order to a treaty for the time being. If any tribe member crossed lines by violating the boundaries outlined on the new map of the island they had drawn up, he or she would do so at his or her own risk. Imprisonment or death would be the penalty for breaking such rules. The wise men agreed to these conditions on behalf of their people and went their separate ways.

Just over a decade after the cease-fire had been ordered, something happened, which no one had foreseen: the young and beautiful daughter of Chief Kodu, Resina, fell in love with the young and handsome son of Chief Feldor.

His name was Akeen and he was a great and fierce warrior, although he was but eighteen. Akeen was out hunting one day, alone in the thick of the island's jungle. He knew exactly where the boundaries of his tribe ended and where the other, hated tribe's began.

Unfortunately, Resina had little talent in the area of remembering boundaries and the like, and happened to cross the lines by a few yards. Though it seemed so miniscule, crossing the lines even an inch deserved a severe punishment. After all, the boundaries were set by the wise men to keep the tribes at bay and from killing each other in entirety. Resina also failed to notice eyes that were watching her. She happily engaged her attentions to the beautiful and bright flowers on the jungle floor. Knowing which ones were beneficial and healing, versus ones that were poisonous, was her gift. Though she knew it was forbidden to sing, she risked humming a simple melody. After all, she was alone— rather, *thought* she was alone—and hummed away, just as happy as the rainbow-colored birds above her.

Akeen, with a spear clenched tightly in his left hand and raised above his head, was ready to attack. But he had never heard something as beautiful or seen someone so beautiful either. His heart melted and he forgot all about the punishment he intended to inflict on the innocent, young woman. Instead, he only thought of speaking to her. It would be worth the possible anger of his father—that is, if his father ever found out.

The young warrior made a split-second decision and jumped down from the tree branch that served as his hidden perch. Resina made a loud gasping sound, surprised by the olive-skinned and handsome man who landed but ten feet from her. Since she had been squatting low to get close to the flowers, her shock propelled her to the ground. Her intuition told her she need not fear him, but she remained frozen and uncomfortable.

Akeen chuckled, "I apologize, I did not mean to frighten you," he said, offering his hand to the beautiful, tanned girl. She hesitated, starting to reach towards him, but let her hand drop back down to the dirt and leaves. "You are right to be cautious—maybe even afraid of me—but I promise I do not bite."

"I do not fear you," Resina answered confidently.

"But I do not know if I should trust you. Are you not of Feldor's tribe? Should you not stay in the boundaries of your own tribe?" Though she became slightly defiant, this only intrigued Akeen further, rather than agitate him.

"You are in the territory of *my* tribe," he replied in a patronizing tone. "Perhaps you need to work on your directional skills, no?"

"I...I..." Resina could only stutter. At this point, she was so taken by the young man, that for the first time in her life, she had little to say. So, she began to laugh. Akeen was now the one in shock. "I suppose you are right," she said with a beautiful smile.

"My father says I do not have the gift of direction. My brother does, however, and it suits his purpose as a warrior. I would rather pick herbs and flowers and use them for the good of my tribe."

Akeen smiled back, making a small chuckle. He extended his hand again and this time, Resina reached up to take it. When their hands met, they both felt a somersault in their stomachs. He pulled her a little too abruptly and she nearly touched his body once she was on her feet. She stumbled back again when she looked into his eyes, but his reflexes kicked in and he secured her once more.

"Thank you," she replied quietly. He was still holding her wrist in one hand and lightly touching her elbow with the other. "Are you ever going to let me go? Or am I to be your prisoner now?" she raised her eyebrows and her eyes caught the beams of sunlight that filtered through the jungle canopy.

"If I can help it, I never want to let you go," he whispered.

"Well, if you do not want to allow me to leave, you should at least ask who I am—and who my father is. That might change your mind," she said, a little more serious this time. Akeen temporarily came back to his senses and countered her suggestion.

"Perhaps I should tell you who *my* father is, before I ask of yours. Perhaps *your* mind will change upon hearing this information. I am Akeen, son of Feldor." He beamed with pride as his announcement that he was a chief's son was made know to the young woman in front of him. She did not seem very impressed, however. Her expression said exactly what she was thinking at that moment: *What, that's it?*

"Hmm...that *does* change things a little. For you see, I am Resina, daughter of Kodu. How interesting that the son of a chief has captured the daughter of another chief. What do you suggest? I come with you quietly until an uprising occurs and our tribes are slaughtered?"

Now she sounded bored. But still, Akeen could not bear to see go—at least, not like this. There was something about this girl. Something he wanted to discover. Perhaps there was a way. He had to see if she would be willing to break the rules.

"Resina," he said, careful to correctly articulate her name. "Yes, I know of your father and I do not doubt he would send every last one of his warriors after you. But perhaps there is a better way."

"Oh?" She finally sounded curious. She could not help but get lost in the warmth of his eyes and noticed how soft his lips appeared while they were moving. "What do you suggest?"

"I will free you, but you must meet me here again tomorrow—at the same time. Maybe we can make an arrangement so I don't have to take you as a prisoner." Now he was simply teasing her. "You can show me what you know of the herbs and flowers. You have my word that I will not scare you again by jumping in front of you." He held his hand to his heart. She appreciated the gesture and knew he was sincere.

"Very well," she replied nonchalantly. "I will meet you here again in one day's time." Just as she turned to leave, he gently grabbed her left hand and brought it to his lips.

"Until we meet again, Resina." He let her hand go and watched her walk away slowly. Then he considered just how much trouble he would be in if it was ever found out that he let someone from another tribe go free— especially the daughter of a chief. His father would have said they could have used her to make demands of Kodu. However, Akeen had a good heart and he knew that whatever the disagreement was between all the tribes, it was not good for the island. Perhaps Resina and he could be the ones to change the way the tribes were. Perhaps.

The next day, the young warrior restlessly paced

the jungle floor. *She's late...maybe she will never come,* Akeen thought. He sighed quietly and sauntered away, a look of defeat on his face. Within seconds, he heard the rustling of leaves and turned around, his spear in an attack position.

"Are you trying to end me again?" the young woman asked teasingly.

"Resina!" Akeen dropped his spear to the ground and ran to greet her. "I thought...well, you were late and...I thought you were never going to come." He gave her a look that beckoned her to encourage his pursuits.

"I am sorry. That was not my intention to make you think that or make you wait for a long time. I had to sneak away. My brother thought I was acting strangely and tried to warn me to be careful about where I was going in this jungle. He especially reminded me to not cross into enemy territories. I had to listen to his lecture to make sure he wouldn't follow me." She grabbed his hand tenderly and said, "Come, let me show you what I know of the flowers and their magic."

Many days passed and each brought a secret, romantic meeting between the two young islanders. Resina, though taken with Akeen, allowed her affections to grow more slowly than his. She understood that they were breaking all the rules of the tribes. And who knew what disaster that could bring if they were ever found out? However, her heart began to weigh heavier than her logic and she found herself falling in love with the handsome young man who spoke tenderly to her, made her laugh, and made her want to sing. As she sat on a tree branch, lost in thought while waiting for him, her thoughts were interrupted.

"Good day, beautiful Resina!" Akeen practically shouted. She laughed and jumped down from the low hanging branch.

"Shh! Do you want us to be discovered?" she scolded, while pressing her finger to his lips. He smiled and grabbed her hand with his right, using his left arm to encircle her waist and pull her close. She looked into his dark, brown eyes and finally felt what he had been declaring for days to her: love. With her free hand, she caught him unawares by grabbing the back of his head passionately, drawing his lips to hers. At first, their kiss was gentle, but it turned into something fierce, heated, and long. When their lips finally parted, Akeen was breathing hard.

"Be my wife," he whispered, putting his forehead to hers.

"Akeen...I want to say yes, I truly do, but...what about the discord between our tribes? Between all the tribes for that matter? Don't you think this will cause another war? Maybe we should run away to the mainland, or—"

"No! Don't you feel it?" He cut her off. "I believe we are the key to changing this island and its people. Our love will be enough to bring everyone together once more. Do you not want that—for all to be united in harmony without these ridiculous boundary lines? It must stop somewhere. We have to try." Though she was scared, Resina knew that something had to change. After all, hadn't she also had the *same* ideas as Akeen just days before? It was worth a try and perhaps this was the way to mend what was broken. She inhaled deeply.

"You are correct; we must try. I think we should begin with my father. He is actually very tender hearted and will listen to me. After my mother died some years ago, he has fulfilled my every wish. I believe he will at least hear what I have to say about this. Besides," she continued while caressing his cheek, "I can be very persuasive when I want to be. All it takes is a simple concoction of flowers."

Chapter Two: The Brotherhood

Eleven figures surrounded a long, rectangular table in a small cottage, hidden in a forest—six men and five women. Some still donned heavy, hooded cloaks splattered with mud, only just arriving from a long journey. The sun sat low on the horizon and the promise of night loomed near. All windows were drawn tight and two men stood watch out front, as heralds, should anyone happen upon the secret meeting inside. There were others in the room; short, stubby-looking creatures with flat foreheads, random patches of hair, and dark, amber-colored eyes, busy serving their guests. One of the female creatures asked the eldest gentleman, "More beer, Dural?"

"No, thank you, Vanchma. You've done enough for us now; I think we have been well taken care of. Please, rest with your family. We have work here to discuss." Vanchma gave him a slight bow and he nodded his head. She exited the small room with the rest of her family, giving Dural and the others privacy. Once the room was quiet, the eldest woman, Ingla, began the meeting.

"I now call this meeting of the Brotherhood to

order," she said with authority. Though she had long, white hair that was braided and pinned close to her head, Ingla looked very young for her seventy years. Her face barely held a wrinkle; her dark green eyes were clear and lively, and her voice was strong and clear. She always sat erect and could wield a sword just as well as any of her younger counterparts. All eyes were on her and her alone.

"Thank you for traveling such a great distance. I know many of you are very tired and we will rest soon. However, you have all received the message and there are things to be attended to. *He*," here, she put a significant emphasis on the word, "has returned. Goden shall be here soon and has word for all of us. The stars have told of his coming and now the signs are no longer a foreshadow, but reality."

"Yes, the prophecies have come to pass," Dural began to speak. "The evil days will no longer be. Hope has returned. There is only one prophecy yet to be fulfilled." He paused, stroking his greying goatee. "Some of you may still have doubts, especially since you have not yet met *him*. However, you have come this far and have been loyal, so I encourage you to pay close attention to every word that Goden has for us. Yes, we are keepers of the Prophecy, but we are also in Goden's service—you will all do well to never forget that."

He specifically lingered his attentions on two of the youngest members: a young man, Ethalo, and a young woman, Tuni. The two noticed and quickly exchanged a glance. Dural continued.

"We expect him any moment..." His words trailed off when one of the men standing guard popped his head through the front door. "Yes? Trouble?"

"No, sir. He's here."

"Please, show him in." Though everyone at the table remained silent, the excitement of having this particular visitor could be felt in the air. An unseen energy swept through the room and the doorway framed someone new: Goden. Everybody stood when he entered.

"Hello, trusted friends," he said warmly. "I do not have much time, so this will be brief. Please, have a seat. As you know, the times have become even more dismal under the reign of the Evil One. But, as you also know, the Prophecy stands and there is nothing he can do about it. Yes, he can try to fight it, but things will inevitably fall in place. The lands can only withstand this imbalance for so long. The time is closer than ever— the Redeemers will be here soon, but you need to understand: they cannot deliver this planet without help.

"Therefore I need a few of you to prepare for their arrival. Are you all familiar with Sikuku Island?" All nodded. "Good. Those who volunteer to go must first help the tribes, who have much discord between them, to make amends. After that, they must learn the ancient, alien language, which will be the only language the Redeemers will speak. You have all been trained for this. Now, the time is here; do your best as we all prepare for hope to reign over Cantelia once more." When he finished their detailed instructions, he looked at each Brotherhood member in the eye, giving a warm smile. "I am sorry we can't have more time together, but that can wait for later. I must take my leave."

"Goden?" asked one of the younger members, Koria.

"Yes?" he answered, turning around to face her.

"Is it *truly* time? How can we know for sure?" Some of her companions, shocked by her forthright question, mumbled to one another in disbelief. How could she have asked such a thing? But Goden only smiled, mirth dancing in his eyes.

"Simply look at the stars, child. They clearly show that it is time. Stars never lie." And with that as a farewell, he quickly exited the cottage and vanished into the night.

Ingla looked at the door fondly and spoke quietly, "It sounds like we have much work to do. Who can I trust to send to Sikuku?"

It was midnight and the room remained dark except for a glowing, blue light in a shiny, silver basin. Someone hunched over the liquid, speaking in a sort of chant. As the chant grew in volume, the liquid transformed, revealing vague images that gave few answers. The chanting stopped abruptly.

"My Lord?" asked a timid voice. "Did you find

anything?" The figure moved in response to the question, but the asker could not see any features, only shadows and perhaps a slight reflection in his eyes.

"Silence!" his voice boomed. "I am thinking." The figure began to pace the room, talking more to himself than his companion. "It seems that I have kept a blind eye on the Sikuku Island for far too long. Those ignorant savages have drafted another peace pact over some ridiculous love story. How pitiful!" He chuckled deeply, but there was no humor in his tone. He continued.

"They can have their peace for a while, until they are cursed. The tribe that has invited in those followers of...of *him*..." here, he held a disgusted look on his face as if someone suggested he eat mealworms and molded bread for dinner. However, his face was still hidden by the darkness and his advisor could not see this. "...will be the tribe most punished and—most likely to be enlisted in my service. Yes, I think I shall enjoy watching them all writhe in pain at their losses. We have much work to do; much work indeed."

Chapter Three: Group Project

There was nothing really special about the morning. The heat of summer was slowly fading. However, it *was* the first day of fall—my favorite season. Plus, it also happened to be Thursday, my favorite day of the week.

People have always asked me, "Why is your favorite day Thursday? Shouldn't it be Friday or a weekend day?" To which I always replied, "Thursday is the most hopeful day of the week; it means that there's a Friday. And if there's a Friday, then there's a weekend." I dunno, I guess it sounded weird but I didn't really care. Having the beginning of fall and Thursday coincide was like getting an unexpected gift.

I walked slowly to the school bus stop, caught up in my daydreams, enjoying the fresh, crisp air of the morning, watching for any sign of leaves changing colors. I put my left hand in one pocket of my favorite faded jeans and started zipping up my knitted, cinnamon brown sweater with my right. A slight breeze rustled my stubby ponytail, tickling my neck. As I continued my slow shuffle, lost in thought, my eyes darted to the right and landed on the approaching figure.

"Alexandra Hill! Why on earth are you moving so slowly? We're gonna be late, girl!"

I began laughing softly at the olive-skinned girl who was giving a scornful look in my direction. "Danielle, stop freaking out! The bus never comes on time anyway. If it makes you happy, I'll pick up the pace."

Danielle had a hard time keeping the frown on her face and shook her head. She rolled her dark, almost black eyes at me.

"Girl, what am I going to do with you? You're crazy, you know that?" The tone of her voice was light and teasing as she fell into step with me, while we finished our walk to the school bus stop. I couldn't help but laugh again.

It was exciting to have started high school with her, especially because we had become best friends in junior high. Dutifully inseparable, we managed to manipulate nearly identical class schedules for the school year by charming our counselor. I think we told him that Danielle had anxiety issues and he bought it. Shady, I know. But hey, it worked.

As I thought about this after exiting the bus, we passed the ghetto, tagged "Pollock Pines High School" sign on the front lawn and made our way to first period. Like clockwork, the day flowed smoothly and before I knew it, lunch came and went. Same ole, same ole. I told Danielle that I'd meet her after school and exited the cafeteria, making my way to Honors English—the only class I had without her. I didn't mind, however; my last class of the day was somewhat tolerable.

Mrs. Brown, our teacher, was known to be eccentric at times—according to the upper classmen—but thoroughly knowledgeable, making the material interesting and the otherwise depressing atmosphere pleasant. In fact, she was probably the only teacher I really liked. A sweet, jasmine scent filled my nose when I approached the gray concrete building—my favorite smell in the world. Besides fresh laundry, of course. I inhaled deeply once more before twisting the knob on the classroom door labeled D-2, pulling it open. *Here I go, back into the 1970s...*

The room smelled of dry erase markers, shampooed carpet and aged wood. Not even *close* to my favorite smells. I wrinkled my nose in disgust. Dark wood panels on the walls didn't help reflect the fluorescent lights effectively, creating diffused light throughout the room. A lack of windows only contributed to the darkness of the drab room. The carpet was burnt orange and extremely outdated. A large, black podium stood at the front of the classroom and a high, squared stool was placed right next to it.

On the wall hung a whiteboard with notes and homework assignments from the previous class period.

The desks were as ancient as the carpet, arranged in neat rows. The shape, size and color of each were just as varied as a bag of trail mix. Not the most modern setting, obviously. With limited public school funding, the whiteboards were the only new addition to most outdated classrooms on campus.

Walking to my assigned seat, I glanced to the back corner of the room and caught Ben Thompson and Lydia Snippens making out. *Ugh. Spare me. Don't they have any regard for those of us with weak stomachs?* Everyone else tolerated them, but I was judging. I guess there were just some things I was taught to keep from the public eye and I didn't care if that made me look like a prude.

I tried my best to ignore them and plopped down in my seat, taking out a green, spiral-bound notebook. Since there were still a few moments left before class, I aimlessly doodled in it. The door opened a few seconds later, and my eyes automatically traveled up to the front of the room to see who would enter. Big mistake.

Although my gaze was friendly and innocent (well, hopefully it was friendly and innocent), the one that met mine was the extreme opposite. It was a scowl that belonged to dark blue and angry eyes. Geoffrey, the so-called "black sheep" of the entire freshman class, entered the classroom and raised one eyebrow to emphasize his annoyance.

"What're you looking at?" he said in a threatening and hellish tone, while taking his seat that happened to be right next to mine. I dropped my eyes quickly, feeling an uncomfortable heat sensation surfacing to my cheeks. My palms became sweaty as I made fists, my heart rate slightly elevated. These things might have signaled embarrassment or humiliation for most girls, but I'm not like most girls. I was mad.

No, *mad* didn't capture my feelings at all. Quite frankly, I was thoroughly agitated, livid and pissed-off. *Seriously, what's his problem? What's so appealing about being a jerk when you're gorgeous and fawned over?* He was never kind or in a good mood for that matter. I bit my tongue to keep from asking him my questioning thoughts out loud. He had problems being humane and I had problems being tactful.

I thought, along with others, that Geoffrey Mitchell was certainly the biggest jerk at school. He was certainly the most attractive person too. All that I heard about him were rumors that he had served time in Juvenile Hall and that his mom was in the state penitentiary for some undisclosed crime. Like mother, like son I guess.

At fifteen, he was older than all our peers—held back in the fifth grade—I had heard someone say before. His jet-black hair had that "messy-yet-sexy" look. Deep, ocean-colored eyes, flawless bone structure and full lips graced his face. I was jealous of his zit-free skin. He was in great shape too. If he had one ounce of benevolence in him, he would have been the perfect guy.

He always kept to himself and became aggressive if anyone made him uncomfortable (and it seemed that *everything* made him uncomfortable). In the first week of school, the students at Pollock Pines High quickly learned to steer clear of him. Still, many girls couldn't help but wish his more than unfriendly manner would melt away to reveal a soft spot so they could stand in line as girlfriend candidates.

Though I was still fuming from his response, I felt silly and stupid at the same time. See, I actually dared to think the same thing as the other girls. *Even if he wasn't rude and anti-social, I'm sure he'd never go for an average-looking girl like me.* There was nothing even remotely perfect about my features. I was a five-foot-three, braced-faced, frizzy-haired nerd. The only thing going for me was my intelligence. But I didn't think striking, fifteen-year-old delinquents were attracted to that.

In fact, I knew they weren't attracted to that and the words of my mother seemed to echo through my mind: *Alexandra, make sure you find a nice guy who puts you first and treats you right.* As cliché as her advice was, I mentally agreed and put those silly thoughts behind me. Sighing quietly, I continued doodling in my notebook, trying to release my anger.

Feast Island

While I finished analyzing his reaction, the rest of the students made their way in right before the late bell rang. Mrs. Brown was already seated at the front of the room on the stool, her posture erect and her deep, jade green eyes dancing from face to face. The heaped and massive coil of honey blonde hair on the top of her head almost overwhelmed her small and defined facial features. She wore black-framed, designer glasses and a smart pink tweed suit.

I think she was around thirty years old, but she seemed ageless and oddly out of place in the dreary classroom—almost as if she belonged somewhere else. She also did not look like she belonged in our small town of Pollock Pines.

"Okay, settle down class," said Mrs. Brown in a calm and cool voice. Her tone immediately sedated the entire room.

"As I promised earlier this week, your group projects will be assigned today. The research and conclusions your groups come to should be in essay format and your in-class presentations will be five to seven minute video clips. You have two weeks to put this project together, meaning I expect to be thrilled when grading your productions." Her last phrase was almost a song and there was a strong emphasis on the word *thrilled*. Slight groans could be heard as she announced the details. The noise seemed to escape her notice and she continued.

"Now, I will read off your group placements.

Please gather together once your name has been called. Group one: Jessica, A.J., Julia, Leyla, Chris, and Rebecca. Group two: Naomi, Lydia, Jacob, Ana, Freddy, and Jesse. Group three: Greg, Brea, John, Laurée, Michael, and Vanessa. And finally, group four: Ben, Alexandra, Daniel, Justin, Heather, Geoffrey, and Keira."

Great, I said to myself. *How lucky am I to be in a group with freaking Geoffrey? I hope I don't lose my temper and snap at him. He better keep his mouth shut—*

"Hey Alex, we're going over to the corner by the door." A deep voice interrupted my train of thought.

It was Ben speaking, as he passed by my desk. He must have noticed the surprised look on my face while he examined my expression and ruffled his light brown hair. Though slightly out of place, every gelled strand on his head still had a designated spot, making it look like he had just walked out of a JC Penney catalog.

"Are you okay?" he asked, his eyes filled with concern.

"Uh...yeah..." I began, my voice unsure. I cleared my throat before continuing. "I'm fine. Just have a lot on my mind, you know?" I attempted a smile after responding, but could only raise one side of my mouth. I'm sure it looked more like a smirk than a smile. He probably thought I was mental. Why did he make me so nervous?

He flashed me an understanding smile. *Why is he so nice?* I opened my mouth to say more, but Lydia approached just then.

"Benny-boo, don't you think Mrs. Brown would let me switch with one of the others in your group? Or maybe she'd let you join *mine?*" Her voice was syrupy and her eyes anxious. Her tone made me want to vomit. She impatiently twisted strands of her long, highlighted hair. Her other hand was resting on her fat-free hip. I rolled my eyes and didn't try to hide it.

"Babe, I don't think Mrs. Brown would let us do that. I mean, she specifically *assigned* us groups so she probably wants us to stay where we've been put. Don't you think?" He gave her a quick peck on the cheek and squeezed her hand.

"I guess so..." She was still apprehensive but turned around, unwillingly, to trudge back to her group. She shot a hateful glance back to me, almost as a look of warning like I was some sort of threat to her. Really though? How could I possibly be a threat to her? It's not like I had a Barbie body too.

Instead of retaliating and speaking my mind, (I was *really* trying to change my obnoxious ways) I attempted to relax and force my features into a more cheerful appearance. I thought it was good enough. Unfortunately, my brain forgot to tell my mouth to keep from blurting out, "Obsessed much?"

I'm sure the look in my eyes became one of horror when it registered that I actually said it *out loud.* At least it wasn't as bad as it could have been. Instead of becoming defensive or irritated, Ben just shrugged.

"Come on. Let's go to our group. They're waiting for us. "

The others had gathered a lumpy circle of desks in the corner by the front door. Most were already chatting among themselves. Of course Geoffrey still maintained a dark countenance and kept to himself by sitting slightly outside the circle. He looked as happy to be in the group as he would be scrubbing gum off the cement in the quad.

Heather Riley, a freckled, tall and slender girl with short strawberry blonde hair and light blue eyes, initiated the group discussion. "I wonder what Mrs. Brown is assigning us for research. I personally would like to investigate the mysteries of the ghost world or zombies. What do you guys think?"

Okay, that's a little weird... Before any of us could answer, Mrs. Brown was standing next to Keira, seeming to appear out of thin air. *How did she do that?*

"For *your* group's assignment, you will be researching and reenacting the legend of our very own lake—Jenkinson Lake, or as locals call it: Spirit Lake. Please examine all the angles of the legend, relate its importance to the Sioux superstitions and develop a contrasting story of your own, using elements of the original.

"Be creative and work as a team—especially

when you film. Most importantly, have fun! This is one of my favorite legends." She smiled briefly, a far off look—or was it a twinkle—in her eye, and turned to walk to another group.

"Are you kidding me?!" complained Keira. Her pouty lips were pursed together while she ran her fingers in a frustrated fashion through her long, silky jet-black hair. Her black brown, almond-shaped eyes swept everyone's faces. "This is the crappiest project ever! Everyone already knows about the stupid legend. It's not even interesting." Her voice was just as irritating as Lydia's.

Even in frustration, Keira Casanoda was beautiful. However, she was one of those girls who knew it too. It was easy enough to hate her for being rich. Her father was the proud and flashy owner of the largest car dealership in El Dorado County, California: Casanoda Imports. Her mother was the head of the city council and pretty much ran our small town of Pollock Pines. Their family had moved here from Sacramento three years ago.

"Who cares if it's not interesting? This is an easy A for sure. Don't know about everyone else, but I'm up for breezing through these next two weeks." The husky voice that answered Keira's outburst belonged to blonde hair, blue-eyed Daniel Kerry.

He was the typical jock who happened to be gifted in academics. He flashed a bright white smile in her direction, but she only sulked more. Gosh, he was such a flirt. His awkward and completely opposite, fraternal twin Justin, couldn't agree more with him.

"I'm with you, D-Dan." He stuttered in a nervous tone, as if the rest of the group might object, throw rotten cabbage at him, and side with Keira. I would probably have stuttered too if I were wearing the retainer which graced his mouth—poor guy.

"This is going to be a piece of cake. In fact, we could film it all this afternoon, combine our research and notes into an essay and get it done and over with. I can shoot and edit the video for us," he suggested. He adjusted his glasses and looked hopeful. But then he immediately looked so unsure and cowering that I wanted to pat his shoulder and tell him it would be okay. He wiped his clammy hands on his jeans as his eyes searched the rest of the group, waiting to hear a response to his offer. Ben countered it.

"I don't think we can get it all done today..." he began. Justin's eager face suddenly fell. "Maybe we should divide the sections into tasks for each of us to do...I dunno—make some kind of list to make it fair." He was moving his hands as he spoke.

"Well, we should write an outline first," I interrupted. "We can plan more from that point and get a better idea of what needs to be done." *Duh.* Shooting a glance at Justin, I added, "I do think we should begin some of the filming today too." What I really wanted to say was, *"Let's get it done and over with, as soon as possible."* I hated group projects like I hated cleaning the toilet. The faster we could get the assignment done, the less painful.

After a few seconds of murmurs, the whole group agreed to let me make my point. We began drafting an outline, tossing ideas back and forth. Before class was over, we came to the conclusion that filming would begin in the afternoon at the lake. Justin would bring his video camera and Daniel would direct the filming. Ben's grandfather owned a small motorboat that we could use to get several angles of the shore from the lake itself. Plus, it would be fun to spend an hour or so on the water.

Everyone had something to contribute to the project—even Geoffrey and Keira went along with the final outline for the project. When the dismissal bell rang, we confirmed that we would meet at the southeast shore by the dam around four.

Chapter Four: The Lake

"Alright, it's settled then. See you all soon." I began to leave my desk and pack my bag, but Mrs. Brown caught my eye and motioned for me to come over to the vintage desk in the corner of the room. The others did not stay to hang out and quickly exited the classroom. Lucky jerks.

"Yes, Mrs. Brown?"

"Alexandra, do you know what today is?"

"Um, the first day of fall?" I guessed. *What is she trying to get at?*

"Well, yes. But that's not really what I meant. It's the anniversary of the legend I assigned your group. You know, they say that on this day, the two fated lovers in the story can be seen walking around the lake at dusk—it's the only time the warrior can see his true love. During the rest of the time, he is guarding the secret of the lake."

Geez, I heard Mrs. Brown was kinda weird, but seriously?! That superstitious? I tried to look politely interested. Besides, I knew the legend anyway and didn't see the point she was trying to make. Much to my dismay, she seemed to read my thoughts and answered them.

"Now, I'm not a superstitious person, Alex. I just wanted to give you a little more background to consider for your research. I find it interesting that you are going to film at the lake *today*, of all the days to do it. Who knows?" she chimed. "You might even see the ghosts themselves." She laughed lightly and gave me a wink and reassuring smile. "I'll be anticipating a very intriguing, updated legend from your group. Please let me know if there's anything you need help with on this project. You have such potential with creative assignments and I know you'll shine in this one." She winked at me again.

"Uh...thanks Mrs. Brown." I looked down slightly and fiddled with my bag strap.

"Now, off you go. Remember to work together."

I was only too glad to be released, my blood throbbing through the veins in my cheeks from the embarrassment of Mrs. Brown's compliment. I mean, I wasn't *amazingly* talented in the creativity department. I only thought of myself as a dabbler in all things creative. Nothing special. She probably had said everything as a way to apologize for putting me in a group with Pouty Princess (Keira) and the Devil's Apprentice (Geoffrey. Obviously).

"Oh, and Alex?"

"Yeah?" I half turned.

"Do be careful if you go out on the lake. The

wind can be tricky sometimes and the sun will set earlier today." Her tone was very grave.

I nodded and turned the handle on the door, anticipating the fresh, sweet air waiting for me. I gulped in the clean oxygen and exhaled through my mouth in relief. Danielle was standing right outside the building.

"What took you so long?" she asked impatiently.

"Oh, uh...Mrs. Brown just wanted to give me more information about our group project." I didn't want to explain how weird I thought the encounter was.

"You have to do a group project? Ew."

"I know. I seriously hate group projects. Actually though, I think it's going to be pretty cool—the project itself, that is. We have to examine the legend of Spirit Lake. In fact, my group begins filming today at four, so we better start moving. I don't want to be late. Oh, and guess who's in my group?!"

We began a brisk walk to the waiting school bus and gossiped about the day. Danielle couldn't believe the tools who populated my group. I told her how Geoffrey was the biggest shocker. When I reenacted the staring incident, she crinkled her brow.

"He *said* that? Why is he so rude? I'm surprised you didn't say anything back." She was giving me a knowing look while rearranging her curly ponytail.

"I know. I had to bite my tongue and believe me—it wasn't easy. I think I was so flustered from his reaction, combined with his gorgeousness, that I only felt temporary confusion." Even Danielle belonged to the group of closet-let's-drool-over-Geoffrey-even-though-he's-a-jerk girls, so she could empathize.

"Ha, ha...well you can stare at him all afternoon. Just make sure he isn't looking." Danielle snickered and I rolled my eyes. We walked for a few blocks before parting ways and gave the usual hug to say goodbye.

The light breeze from the morning was slowly and steadily becoming heavier. A gust of wind blasted through the trees, sending chills through my body. I walked quickly to warm up. It helped some, but then I recalled the conversation I had with Mrs. Brown before leaving campus. There was this feeling I couldn't shake—the feeling that something about our chat was off....*Nah*, I thought.

Without formulating other ideas to contribute to my already wild imagination, I popped in my earplugs, played one of my favorite songs on my iPod and trudged up the road that led to my house. Though I had a house key, I didn't need one. The front door was unlocked as usual and I waltzed right in to our short hall. Believe it or not, there are still some places left in the world where you don't need to lock your doors and windows.

We lived toward the end of a tucked away neighborhood in Sly Park Hills. The house belonged to my grandma. When my grandfather had passed away

41

three years ago, my family and I had moved in with her to help take care of the house and really, just to keep her company. Sometimes it was hard to see the pictures of my grandfather still around. We had been very close and I missed him very much.

Dad lived there with us too, but not full-time. He usually stayed at our house in San Bruno because his job kept him there most days out of the month. He's a firefighter and since it helps to pay the bills, he stayed put. Plus, his transfer request to Pollock Pines had been denied. So we all made do, though it was difficult at times.

Mom kept busy as the manager of the only grocery store in town—Safeway—and my sister, Lauren, worked part-time at the Starbucks in the store. She was in her senior year of high school this year and couldn't wait to leave our town and go far away to this confectionary school, where they trained people how to become chocolatiers and pastry chefs.

Pollock—which was a shortened name we used—was growing on me and I liked the more quiet and laid-back life of the mountain and forest area. I liked hearing nothing but cricket chirps and wind at night. There were wind chimes that made sleepy, familiar sounds right outside the bedroom window my sister and I shared, reminding me of my childhood. I liked going for hikes with Danielle around the lake every now and then.

When it snowed, it was fun to go sledding down

the steep hills around the neighborhood—when we had enough snow, of course. I had been skiing since the age of four and loved going to the winter resorts off Highway 50 with my family during the winter.

Once in a while, a wild turkey or deer would enter our backyard. The most positive thing about moving though, as far as I was concerned, was the hot tub out on the back deck. We often went in it when the sun was setting and chatted about our day while relaxing.

When I entered the kitchen, I threw my school bag on the table and turned around to face the counter. I was pretty sure my sister was out with her boyfriend, and my brother, Sean, was in the RV that functioned as his bedroom. Talk about one spoiled sixteen-year-old. At least he had to stay out of mine and Lauren's bathroom.

Mom and Grandma weren't home yet either, so being the responsible child (unlike my older siblings), I scribbled a quick note to her since she didn't text a lot:

Went to the lake for a group project. Should be home by dinner.

Have my cell if you need to call. Love ya, Alex

I stuck the note to the fridge with one of my grandma's Shi Tzu magnets and opened the door to grab some string cheese. While I chewed on it, I thought about the project soon to commence at the lake. If we were all going to be *in* the video, I needed to at least put some gel in my out-of-control hair that had turned into a frizzy nest, thanks to the wind. I walked to the bathroom and looked in the mirror.

Hopeless. I sighed at my reflection, wishing that the confident person I felt inside matched the girl who stared back at me. My reddish brown mop was a mess. I still had no idea how to control the curls that tried so hard to surface. Maybe I didn't have the right products, maybe I lacked talent, maybe the fates destined me to have frizzy hair forever—just like that Magic School Bus teacher, Ms. Frizzle. At least I didn't have crazy shoes like her too.

My eyes could have been a pretty green, but they were never able to decide if they wanted to be brown, hazel or green. The result was a muddy-looking olive tone. My face was round and sort of pudgy—does that count as baby fat still if you're fourteen? The freckles on my cheeks and nose matched the red in my hair and what little tan I managed to get this summer was fading fast, making them brighter than I wanted. I guess I could have put on some make-up but didn't know where to begin. My lips were the same size on the top and bottom and were stretched out abnormally because of my stupid braces.

Like I said, hopeless. Unless I turned into some kind of a supermodel overnight, I didn't think that the remainder of puberty would do much else for me other than add a few inches of height (hopefully) and grant me some visible cheekbones. Oh, and maybe some boobs too, instead of the mosquito bites I had. Talk about depressing. I sighed again, put some gel on all the flyaways and moistened my eyes with drops. *Well, this is as good as it's gonna get.*

I left the small bathroom and headed back to the kitchen. My notebook was probably the only thing I would need, so I excavated it from my bag. I put my glasses' case in my jacket pocket.

It would be cold on the lake, and I would need to bundle up. Mom had taken our winter gear out of storage already, so I grabbed a scarf and beanie from the coat rack in the hall. Taking a deep breath, I reached for the door handle on the front door and stepped out. I went in the garage, mounted my bike and started my journey to Spirit Lake.

I took the neighborhood streets down to the main road, Sly Park Road, appreciating the view of the surrounding fields. The horses were out, eating grass to their hearts' content. I pedaled faster on the same road on which my grandma had just begun to teach me how to drive. With my birthday coming up, I only had to wait another fourteen months until I could get my license. I was learning how to drive my grandfather's yellow, stick shift Jeep Wrangler but wasn't terribly great just yet. Finally, Mormon Immigrant Trail Road was to my right and I took the turn. I found the entrance to the trail easily, chained my bike to a tree and made my way down the trail.

The twins were already on the dirt and mud beach. I waved when they noticed me approaching on the trail; Daniel smiled in response and Justin nodded. They were busy looking through all the camera equipment, probably deciding what to use, given the already fading sunlight. I assumed Ben was getting the boat ready with his grandfather. Hopefully everyone else would be on time.

I turned to face the glistening green and blue water. It was extremely beautiful in the afternoon light. Not a cloud was in the sky. You could still see some snow on the very tops of the Sierra Mountains and the wind blasted a sweet, pine scent to my nose. There weren't a whole lot of people around. In fact, most visitors were beginning to bring their boats in from spending the day on the lake. The dock was growing more crowded.

Just then, I noticed Heather walking toward me. The poor girl was tripping on the roots along the trail as if she didn't know they were present. Never before had I observed someone who lacked so much grace in her stride. It was almost painful to watch.

Maybe her long limbs were too much for her and she didn't know what to do with them. I couldn't understand how she managed to stay on her feet. I ran up the trail to help her come down the somewhat steep incline.

"Hey, Alex," she said with a tone of gratitude.

"Hey, Heather. Tricky roots, huh?" I tried to sound lighthearted.

"Oh yeah...I'm pretty clumsy. Ha, ha." Her

laugh had a sarcastic tone. "My mom joked that even if I lived in an unbreakable bubble, I'd find some way to destroy it." With that explanation, I knew she didn't mind my teasing, so I pressed my luck further.

"Ouch...Well I hope you don't tip the boat over today." I winked to disclaim actual seriousness.

She responded by biting her lip and looking down. "Actually, Alex, I hope I don't either. I've had past incidents..."

I blinked in confusion, not sure how to respond. She studied my face.

"I'm just kidding! I didn't think you'd believe me." She grinned at me, displaying a set of perfect, white teeth. *Showoff.*

"Oh...uh, good one." *Awkward...* "We'd better catch up to Daniel and Justin and get the four-one-one." I gestured to the twins.

"Right. Let's go." We walked up to the boys, Daniel again greeting us with a smile.

"Hi ladies! You ready for some fun?" He said *fun* like it was the word of the day.

"Ben's at the dock. He and his grandpa are getting the boat ready for us take out. We just need Geoff and Keira." *Gosh, he sure is chipper. Where can I get the happy pills he takes?*

We saw someone coming shortly after he spoke; it was Geoffrey. He didn't look as angry but he still looked like he could be easily annoyed. I decided to avoid eye contact with him completely—just in case.

He nodded at Daniel and said in a rude tone, "I just saw Her Highness"—he made quotations with his fingers when saying that—"being dropped off in a BMW. I'm surprised her zillionaire daddy didn't pay the fee and drop her off at the dock parking lot." Daniel snorted and shook his head.

"Ben's at the dock. As soon as Keira gets here, let's head over. We should get shots of the water and shore first before we lose too much light."

Heather and I continued to make small talk, me asking her about her home in Los Angeles and what she thought about moving north to our small town. I knew it had to be a big and possibly unwelcome change. There's not much to do here if you're used to living in the city. Sure, Lake Tahoe's only forty-five minutes east but it wasn't ski season yet and we were all too young to gamble at one of the casinos. With her clumsiness, I didn't think Heather was one for fishing or boating much—or even hiking at that. Geoffrey sat with us—next to me, actually—but didn't say a word and appeared to be disinterested.

"Heather, I just remembered that you live behind us, right? I should have waited to ride here with you. Sorry I didn't think about that," I said.

"It's okay," she replied warmly. "I kinda forgot too. Maybe next time." She smiled at me and we continued to chat. Once I stopped judging her weird comments and unruly coordination, she wasn't half bad. I decided I would try my best to be kind and befriend this interesting girl from Southern California. Perhaps I could gain one friend from this agonizing experience. My relocation experience had been tough at first, but then I got used to living the small town life and was grateful for the friends I had met.

Finally, about ten minutes after Geoffrey's arrival, Keira made it to our site. She didn't shake the pouty, sour look on her face. No one bothered to greet her as she took her sweet time joining the group. I think she was mad that she had to take the trail down. Or maybe she was mad that she had to trade her stiletto boots for practical tennis shoes. Who knew?

"Well..." started Daniel, "We have everyone here, so let's go find Ben."

Ben and his grandfather were just settling everything in the boat when they saw us. "Hey guys! Ready for some fun?" He grinned. "Do we have everything we need? Alex, you brought the outline, right?"

"Yeah." I tried to keep the annoyance in my voice to a minimum. *Hello, I am responsible, thanks.*

"Good. Oh, and by the way, this is my grandpa. Grandpa, this is my group." We all took turns shaking Ben's grandfather's hand. He was a big man with rough but warm hands—hands that clearly knew what hard labor was. He was quiet, but smiled and made eye contact. His mannerisms reminded me of my own grandfather—except for the quiet part. It made me miss him. After the brief introduction, he motioned for us to start climbing aboard.

Ben said, "Okay then guys, watch your step as you get in. Maybe Justin should go first since he has all the expensive stuff."

When we were all cozy in the boat, Ben thanked his grandfather for letting us use it. He told Ben he'd be back in an hour to meet us at the dock when we were finished. We all waved goodbye, Ben started the motor, and we began our journey around the edge of the lake. The wind was beginning to pick up again and I noticed everyone clinging to his or her jacket.

When the boat accelerated to full speed, it would get really chilly. I put my hood on, not caring how ridiculous I looked with the fringes of my scarf sticking out of my jacket like brown-red French fries and my knitted beanie making my head look twice as large as it really was. Too bad I had forgotten to grab my mittens.

Though it was windy, the lake was still relatively calm. Thanks to the dock slowly filling up from the day boaters, we had Spirit Lake almost all to ourselves. I began reviewing the outline, asking the group what shots we needed first. I had to practically yell over the sound of the motor.

We started talking about the legend itself and Daniel interrupted the brainstorming session with a question: "So everyone knows about the legend of the lake, right?"

Heather looked intrigued and asked if he would

tell it since she was only vaguely familiar with the story. Ben slowed down the boat so Justin could begin to take some shots of the shore from the water. Having less noise was the perfect opportunity for Daniel to tell the legend.

I remembered my grandfather telling me about it a few years ago, but couldn't recall all the details. It would be cool to hear it again, especially to help us all out with the project. Daniel's countenance changed as he furrowed his brow and lowered his voice. I suspected that he enjoyed storytelling immensely and that this wasn't his first time telling the account of the Indian, *Star of Day* and his equally fair lover, the *Pale-faced Dove*.

Chapter Five: The Legend

"Many moons ago," Daniel began—I was currently trying to hold in laughter and keep a sober face—"there was a great Modoc warrior-chief in these parts. His tribe revered their god of war and would make sacrifices of human flesh to appease his changing temperament, hoping he would find favor with them.

"The chief and his warriors ransacked the villages of the pale faces and ambushed any travelers unfortunate enough to cross their path. The warriors never intentionally left survivors, except for the one unfortunate soul to be sacrificed on the beach: the sacrifice for the god of war.

"One day, on a typical raid, a beautiful woman was chosen to be the offering. In their haste, the warriors did not notice the bundle she huddled to her chest. When she was brought to the chief, he grabbed it from her, finding a small, beautiful baby under the pieces of cloth.

"He was about to instruct his warriors to sacrifice the infant with its mother, but his wife begged him to let her keep it since she was unable to have

52

children of her own. He relented, but only under one condition: that he would train the male child to be the fiercest warrior the tribe had ever seen. His wife hastily agreed and took the sleeping baby away from its tear-strewn, screaming mother."

"Okay...wait a minute", interrupted Heather. "Why would the chief's wife take some baby that wasn't Modoc? Weren't they killing all the white people? Didn't they hate them?"

"Well, yeah..." said Daniel patiently. "But the baby was so beautiful that the chief's wife wanted him as her own. Think the story of baby Moses meets American Indian legend."

"Ah, I see. Thanks. Sorry for interrupting." Heather urged him to continue.

"As the pale-faced child grew, he was trained to become the most feared warrior in the land. He was strong, fierce and ruthless, bringing bloody glory to his name and his tribe.

"The chief named him *Star of Day* because he was the beacon of the tribe, his light skin seeming to shine bright as he conquered their enemies.

"As Star of Day was becoming a man, he had just finished ransacking a group of travelers, waiting for one of the warriors to bring the chosen victim-sacrifice over to the chief. When he looked into the light eyes of the chosen one, the pale-faced warrior was caught by surprise.

"When he gazed upon the most beautiful, fair-skinned woman he had ever seen, he felt a surge of emotions coming from his chest—emotions he had never experienced before. Emotions he could not describe or label with words. He suddenly had fear that this woman—this pale-faced dove—would be dead by dawn's light the next day and he would never see her again. The chief appointed him as her guard to make sure she didn't escape. He gratefully attended to his task, planning to release her and take the blame when she was found missing the next morning.

"In the prison hut, the warrior offered her food and she accepted his small offering with a gentle smile and a trusting look in her eyes. He wanted to tell her how beautiful she was and that everything was going to be okay. While they ate their meal in silence, he thought about the innocent lives he had destroyed and wished he could erase the past. Did he yet have time to reclaim his soul?"

"Hold up!" Keira was the next to disrupt the story. "How the heck did the warrior—er, Star of Day or whatever—change his heart so quickly? He had been raised as a complete savage."

Daniel seemed less patient with Keira's question. "Well, love is a magical and powerful thing", he said, almost sarcastically. "Besides, this is a legend and it's not supposed to take *forever* to develop the love connection like fictional romances from the 1800's. Just accept it and let me finish, 'kay?"

"Fine. Whatever. Go ahead." She folded her

arms and looked uninterested. I guess there really are some people who don't appreciate good stories.

"Anyway," he began again, "as the evening wore on, they started to feel the electricity of their attraction to one another. He resolved quickly that he would help this young woman escape by way of the lake. Maybe the spirits guarding the lake would grant them safe passage.

"The full moon shone bright through the window of the little hut on the beach, illuminating her graceful features. He was afraid that if he moved closer to her, she would lose trust in him and shrink away or scream. But he couldn't help himself and decided it was worth the risk, suddenly inching nearer.

"In response, she leaned toward him—as if in encouragement. He could barely breathe and swore he heard her heart beating rapidly. When their lips touched, he felt a surge of desire stronger than any urge he had ever experienced, except the desire to keep her safe. When the night was its blackest, the softened warrior urged the young woman to rest. He lay awake and watched her sleep in his arms."

"See?" Ben was interjecting this time, with a look of mischief in his eyes. "Love is *m-a-g-i-c*." He said the word 'magic' in a drawn out, teasing tone.

"Ben! Shut up and let me finish the freaking story already!"

"Sorry dude, couldn't help myself. Hurry up though; we're almost to the center of the lake." Ben had restarted the motor but was keeping the boat going at a slower pace than our initial launch. Thoroughly agitated, Daniel continued.

"As soon as he could see a hint of light, Star of Day woke his pale-faced dove and they quietly left the hut. At the water's edge, there were several canoes belonging to the tribe. When they were halfway across the lake, they heard a low rumbling noise like thunder. The calm water developed waves that rose higher with every passing minute. A howling wind rattled their eardrums and suddenly, the boat started to spin uncontrollably. The two of them clung to the wood for dear life as they spiraled down a whirlpool in the middle of the lake to their death. Reaching the bottom of the lake, darkness overtook them.

"Moments later, the warrior heard a voice calling, 'Star of Day! Wake up!' He obeyed and opened his eyes to lights that glistened and glittered all around him. He saw the woman a few feet beyond him, lying on her side with her eyes closed. He rushed over to her, gently shaking her shoulders. Her eyes fluttered open. She threw her arms around his neck and crushed his body to hers. 'Where are we?' she whispered, knowing he would not be able to answer her.

"However, a puzzled look consumed his face and he answered, 'I'm not sure.' They could understand each other! She opened her mouth to say more, to really make sure that she was not hallucinating, but a glowing light caught her attention. He saw it too, immediately bringing her to her feet and simultaneously placing his body protectively in front of her. Glowing, ghost-like figures approached the wary couple. Their features were unintelligible and they appeared to float rather than walk.

"The tallest one spoke to them: 'Fear not, Star of Day. We mean you no harm, although no harm can befall you now.' It had the face of a man, maybe an angel—for he was one of the most beautiful people either of them had laid eyes upon. The ghost continued to speak. 'I am the Spirit of the lake and I guard it with the other spirits.' He gestured to the ghosts standing off in silence. 'We saved your spirits before the god of war could claim them.'

"Star of Day threw his hands to his forehead and looked down at the ground, creasing his eyebrows together. He realized that he and his new love *actually* drowned in the whirlpool created by the angry god.

"The spirit seemed to read his thoughts. 'Yes, you are dead...but not at rest yet. I saved your spirit to save your soul from a greater fate than you realize. Because of your dark deeds as a savage warrior, you have a steep price to pay for retribution. If you want your spirit to be put to rest, you must join us in guarding the lake—granting safe passage to those in need and protecting this holding place from evil.

"'When your time is up, you will be put to rest forever with your love. If you choose not to accept my offer and conditions, or should you fail in your tasks, you will be damned and forever separated from the one you cherish.'

"While the reformed warrior heavily contemplated all that had been revealed to him, the young woman broke the silence. 'And what of me? What is my fate?' She stood motionless while awaiting an answer.

"'You, my child, already have a pure soul. Your love has redeemed this heartless man, saving him from eternal darkness. You may choose to enter your rest now or wait here with us while Star of Day completes his duties.'

"Without thought, the young woman answered the spirit. 'I choose to stay here.' The warrior took her hand and responded to the spirit's offer.

"'Great Spirit, I fully accept your terms and will protect this place and the lake to the best of my abilities. I will serve you in hopes that the redemption of my soul will make me even remotely worthy of the goddess who stands by my side.'

"And so it was decided that day; the warrior would protect the holding place of the spirits and guard the lake. Because of her love, the woman would be allowed to visit her reformed warrior every day at sundown, for one hour, until his time had been served in entirety. It is said that to this day, the warrior still serves the spirits of the lake. Every now and then, their ghosts can be seen roaming one of the beaches at dusk when they are allowed to reunite temporarily."

As he finished the story, Daniel relaxed his features and chuckled slightly. "Pretty crazy story, huh?"

"What is so special about the holding place of the spirits? Why must it be guarded?" Heather wondered.

"Well, that's the mystery of the story, I guess", replied Daniel. "No one really knows. Some people have guessed that there's a cave filled with treasure down there or that the 'holding place' holds a secret to eternal life...you know, like the recipe for immortality or something."

"You're a really good story-teller Daniel," I said suddenly. "I've never quite heard it like that before." I admired his passion, wishing I could be half that articulate when giving speeches in class. I was also reminded of what Mrs. Brown said after class: about the ghost lovers strolling around the lake at the end of the day. It made me shiver even though I knew it was an old wives' tale.

"Thanks", he said modestly. "I guess I get it from my dad. He would always tell me and Justin bedtime stories when we were little."

"Camera's ready for some new shots," said Justin. He sure looked anxious to film even more. What a little nerd. I know, I know...takes one to know one.

"Okay. Let's get a wide shot of the shore and the

beaches. It looks like most people have cleared off now." Daniel began directing the project. Everyone glanced toward the beach on the south shore, shielding their eyes with their hands to avoid squinting from the setting sun. Keira quickly equipped her face with Dolce & Gabbana shades. What a snob.

The wind was making a low howling sound almost too soft to notice. Justin pointed the camera in the direction of the beach and gave us warning that he would hit the record button in three, two, one...He panned slowly from the lake to the shore and we all watched quietly in the large viewfinder that was flipped open. Not a person was in sight and the sand and rocks seemed to sparkle in the sunset. He then panned over to the small island about two hundred feet away from the boat and lingered the shot on the beach. When he started to move it back to the water, two specks of something materialized—almost out of thin air.

"Whoa, what's that?" he said. He zoomed in.

"Ah, probably just some squirrels or something", said Geoffrey.

"They're growing bigger though. Maybe they're bear cubs?" suggested Heather.

"There aren't any bears around here, Heather," heckled Ben.

"Hold on, let me zoom in some more," said Justin in a serious tone.

"What in the..." began Justin. The specks were

two blobs now and were gray and black in color, still lacking definite shape.

We all rubbed our eyes in disbelief. The shapes that emerged—yes, *emerged*—were beginning to look, well, *human* but they weren't like that two seconds before. Or were they? We watched closely for a while longer and a man and woman appeared from the shapes.

They had full color now, yet were eerily transparent like ghosts. Not that I'd ever seen an *actual* ghost, but this seemed like the real deal. I wondered if Criss Angel was around, filming some new "Now You See It, Now You Don't" kind of show, but that was highly doubtful.

The sunlight was fading fast—faster than it normally did—and the wind was gaining speed. I didn't know about the others, but my body was paralyzed in shock and fright. Shock more so than fright, I'd say. Then the figures started moving and turning toward us. That's when the fear took over and I thought I was going to pee my pants.

"Is everyone seeing what I'm seeing?" asked Justin, almost in a whisper. No one could respond. We were all so dumbfounded. *Were the two ghosts waving at us?*

The sound of thunder snapped us out of our temporary comas. Ben reacted by shaking his head and opening his eyes wide.

"We need to get out of here guys. Sounds like a

bad storm is coming." I didn't remember any storm warnings for the day. He yanked the pulley to start the motor, but it wouldn't start. He tried again, but to no avail. The boat was a little unstable and gradually started to rock from side to side in a matter of seconds. That's when it happened.

A big wave crashed over the side of the boat, making Keira, Daniel and Heather soaking wet. I looked around and saw one coming to my side now. We all started screaming and yelling. Justin clutched his camera like it was the last piece of food in a starving nation. To my horror, more waves were coming at us on all sides. I gripped the side of the boat with all my might, wondering where the life jackets were in this sardine can. This was *not* the Spirit Lake I knew.

We were all drenched in seconds and the boat started to rock violently up and down. "Make it stop!" I yelled helplessly, knowing it would do no good. I felt myself getting nauseous and everything around me started spinning. I realized that the entire boat was spinning. *What the crap was going on?*

Against my will and control, I started sliding back into Ben. Justin was on a downhill trip towards me and just like dominoes; Geoffrey was slipping toward us too. This was NOT the kind of manwich I liked. The other side mirrored ours, everyone smooshing into one another.

The nose of the boat tipped up and was beginning to point toward the now darkened sky. I could see my brief life flash before my eyes, just like they say happens when you face death, and I held on tightly to Geoffrey's arm while screaming. *Was this really happening right now?!*

The boat was still spinning on its weird angle and it felt like we were being flushed down a toilet. Squeezing my eyes shut, I mentally said a quick and frantic prayer. I could tell exactly when the water finally engulfed us because the screams became muffled.

Holding my breath, I opened my eyes briefly. I tried desperately to swim to the surface, but some kind of gravitational pull was in force and my legs stopped working. My throat started to burn and everything went black.

Chapter Six: Wait...Where Are We??

I was having one of the most vivid dreams. There I was in the night sky, floating in the clouds. My body was weightless and I didn't have a care in the world. It felt so nice to be free like that. I wished it could go on forever and began making swimming motions. But then I heard a deep, booming voice saying, "Alexandra! Wake up!"

Suddenly, a murky light appeared in the darkness and my chest started to feel a tightening sensation. I gulped for air but felt salty wetness hit my tongue, choking back any attempt to inhale some much-needed oxygen.

Still moving in a swimming motion, I intuitively kicked my legs, heading straight for the light. The blackness was slowly changing to a bluish color, the murky light becoming more yellow and scattered. My limbs didn't feel as weightless as before; in fact, they were heavier with each kick—like something was tugging at me. I watched the sleeves on my arms in front of me swish up and down, but with a drag to the movement. That's when it hit me: I was in the water, drowning!

Swim, swim, SWIM, was all I could tell myself. My vision spun and my lungs felt like they were going to explode, but I knew to keep going in the direction of the light. I made one last herculean push toward it to pop my head out of the water.

When my head exploded from the surface, I gasped in air as fast as I could. I was sputtering and half-choking on liquid that seared the lining of my lungs. I needed to get to the shore before my legs gave out. Fortunately, the beach was about fifty feet away in front of me. I mentally thanked my mother for the early childhood swim lessons she dragged my sister and I to every summer at the Y, and swam freestyle to the shore with some ease. I practically crawled up the sandy slope and plopped stomach down with fatigue, breathing hard and fast.

It took me a while to remember everything before that moment. As I replayed the whole ghost-sighting and boat incident in my head, I panicked. *Where are all the others? Did they make it, too?* I sat up and turned my body to face the water. Everything was blurry. *Dang it!* My stupid contacts were too salty from the water! Guess I'd have to resort to glasses. Once my glasses were on—thank goodness they hadn't fallen out of my pocket. After blinking away the rest of the water droplets, I was able to see some figures swimming to the beach.

"Alex! Is that you?" Ben yelled.

He was the closest to the shore out of the others and stood up in the water when he got to the sand. I tried to yell back, but I started coughing, tasting the saltiness again. *Salt? Since when did the lake have salt in it?* He ran to me and kneeled down.

"You okay?" He started to pat my back lightly. I nodded my head while coughing—so attractive. Finally, I was able to respond.

"Yeah, I'm okay. Just trying to get all the water out of my lungs I guess," I said weakly. I couldn't believe how he managed to still look cute after escaping a possible drowning. I knew my appearance probably mimicked that of a wet rat.

He looked relieved and put his hand above his eyes to shade them as he turned away from me and examined the water. When he did that, it dawned on me that the sun was much brighter than before. I was just beginning to wonder why that was so when Ben ran back down to the water to help Heather and Daniel.

Geoffrey was right behind them, seemingly unscathed by the trauma of our boat capsizing. He was half holding, half dragging Keira. I knew she would probably be more upset that her make-up and hair were ruined than the fact that we all had a near death experience. Then I started thinking that Justin would be more upset about his camera...

Wait a minute, where is Justin? I stood up and frantically scanned the surrounding beach and the area in the water behind the emerging teens. My heart froze. My eyes met Daniel's and he saw the worried expression my face wore. He too began to search around us, desperate for a sign of his brother.

"Justin? Justin! You okay bud?" His last question was shaky, but he kept shouting and looking around at the water's edge.

His shouts were fruitless. As the others in my group continued to walk to my landing site, their tired and pale faces began to change to panicked countenances. Everyone was thinking the same thing but didn't want to say it out loud. Instead, we all turned to the water again and cupped our hands over our mouths, joining Daniel's yell-chant for Justin.

"Look! Over there!" pointed Heather.

I strained my eyes even more. There was something floating in the water, being pushed to the shore by the waves. The unmoving form wore Justin's plaid jacket and was face down. *Oh God,* I pleaded internally. *Please let him be okay!* Daniel started to dart for the water, but Ben was faster. He tore off his wet shirt and jumped into the crashing waves, swimming like a...well, like a merman.

He got to Justin in no time and brought him to a hysterical Daniel. We were all huddled around the lifeless, pale blue Justin as Ben felt for a pulse and listened for any signs of breathing. "Geoff, help Dan out, will ya?" Ben ordered calmly.

Daniel was screaming, "Justin! Justin! Wake

up!", like a psycho parent of an ER patient, getting in the way of emergency doctors and nurses trying to save their child. I couldn't blame him for reacting that way though; I can't say I wouldn't do the same. Geoffrey held Daniel back and the girls and I knelt down around Justin and Ben. I was hoping that Ben really knew what he was doing because Justin had less than minutes before possible brain damage or death. The thought made me feel queasy.

"He's not breathing, so watch out guys and stay out of my way; I'm gonna have to perform CPR." Ben's tone was solemn and filled with authority. I guess he *did* know what he was doing after all. *Well, this should be interesting...*

He pinched Justin's nose and tilted his head back to start giving him some air. Two breaths and thirty compressions were given in intervals. After a full set, Ben was watching Justin's chest for a sign of revival. On the third try, he paused after giving him more air. I whispered more prayers and swore I could see Justin's lips start to move and—

"He's okay! He's breathing!" Ben's news somewhat calmed the panic-stricken Daniel and Geoffrey released his hold. Daniel rushed forward to help his brother into a sitting position as the rest of us backed up to give them some room.

"You okay, J? You sure scared me, bro." Daniel's hysteria had calmed a bit and he started to sound relieved.

"Yeah...never better," Justin managed to choke out. He was holding his knees to his chest, breathing hard. He looked like a hot mess—which we all did, but he was worse for the wear. His glasses were missing too. At least his color was returning.

"Hey Ben," he said, still short of breath. "Thanks for saving my life. I...well, I...thought I might not make it." His eyes looked like they were becoming moist and it wasn't because of the water he'd just been pulled out of. His expression reminded me of a little boy who wakes up scared from a nightmare.

"Don't mention it," replied Ben. "I'm just glad I knew what to do. I was a lifeguard at the community pool this past summer and they really put us through some intense rescue and first aid training. Plus, my mom's a nurse and she's taught me a lot about what to do in emergencies."

"Let's get you home, bro." Daniel indicated gratitude to Ben with a nod and both he and Ben started to help Justin to his feet. When Justin was vertical, I started to look around me—like *really* look around—and my heart dropped.

Nothing was familiar at all. For one, the previously sandy and rocky beach was just sand with a red brick color and looked lighter and softer than the stuff on the south shore. I couldn't believe how I'd missed the unusual color, especially when it was the first thing I landed on. It kinda looked like the play sand you buy at a craft store when you make those sand-in-a-bottle projects.

Two, the usual forest-like surroundings were replaced with plants that were right out of the *Jungle Book*—maybe larger and greener though. And three, when I quickly looked back to the water, it was an actual *ocean*—definitely not a lake—not *our* lake. There was no dock and no other signs of life around. *Where were we?* Keira interrupted my internal question with a verbal one.

"Hey—are we even on the south beach?" Her voice trembled with uncertainty and everyone paused his or her activity to look around. Uncomfortable silence blanketed the group like a thick fog. I held my breath, hoping someone had the answer.

"Um...not to sound cliché or anything, but I don't think we're in Pollock Pines anymore," started Ben. Relieved that someone finally spoke, I was encouraged to let out some of my thoughts.

"Obviously NOT! But if we're not at Spirit Lake...heck, if we're not even in Pollock Pines anymore—which I have to agree with you there, Ben— then where are we?"

"The only way to find out is to explore", said Heather, with an excited tone. *How could she possibly be excited? Common sense, much?*

"Agreed," responded Geoffrey. "We're not getting anywhere by staring at each other, so let's get moving *somewhere*, at least. And we really need to find someone to look Justin over." Did he lack common sense too? We didn't know what dangers could have been lurking around.

"Justin, you okay to start walking around?" asked Ben. He was always so considerate! Geez, did he take happy pills too?

"Yeah..." started Justin. "I think I'm okay. Geoff's right—we gotta start looking around so we can get home soon."

After mild deliberation and much to my dismay, the majority voted on heading further down the beach to our left—when we were facing the ocean, that is. Keira was muttering something about having sand in all the wrong places and that her shoes were ruined from the water. Like I cared. At least we were alive. Did she even think about *that* fact?

As we started our search for clues telling us where we were, I surveyed my surroundings again. A million things were running through my head, such as: *Do oceans really twinkle like that?* And *Are jungle plants that lush?* I thought too about how bright it was—wherever we were—which was weird, because the last I remembered before our boat accident was that the sun was setting. I carefully shielded my eyes as I was thinking this and looked up to the bright sun over our heads. I knew that I could only steal a quick glimpse or my eyes would be damaged, so I squinted.

All my other thoughts came to a halt when I noticed that the sun wasn't its usual orange yellow color—it was actually a bright blue mixed with white.

The combination made it almost sparkle, which I imagined was the cause for the ocean's (or whatever) sparkles. Plus, there were actually *two* suns—the ginormous blue one and a smaller, orange red one—resembling the sun I was used to seeing. I could feel a knot in my stomach and turned to the others. *Two* suns?

"Hey, you guys..." I said, my voice shaky. "Did any of you notice the two suns, or am I seeing things?" Immediately, everyone stopped walking and looked at the sky too.

"Whoa!" Justin sounded more fascinated than freaked out—freaked out being the normal response of a sane person when finding their world has completely turned upside down. But everyone in our group, it seemed, was missing the part of the brain that controls common sense.

"Is this a dream?" asked Heather. "Are we having the same hallucination?"

"Well, if you can all see the same blue white colored sun and the orange red sun close to it, then I'd say we're not dreaming or hallucinating," replied Ben matter-of-factly.

"This is really freaky," Daniel began, sounding very unlike the brave young man he always seemed to be. "Do you think it's like the end of the world or something and weird things like that whirlpool in the lake are starting to happen?"

"I don't know what this is," Geoff said. "But I do

know that we need to keep walking if we're ever gonna find some answers. Staring at each other isn't going to get us anywhere."

Everyone was eerily quiet as we continued our journey for what seemed like hours. I was practically starving, but I had a hunch that the empty feeling in my stomach was due to anxiety, stress, and fear more so than hunger pangs. I would have welcomed a cheeseburger at any moment though. The strange suns were dropping lower in the sky. I had this small thought running through my head: *What if we're not on earth?*

Keira stopped complaining about her stupid shoes and actually looked shaken. Geoffrey's face had completely lost its mean look and it was now filled with concern and urgency.

Something weird was going on and we were determined to find out just what. I had a sick feeling in my stomach that the answer we were looking for might be awful—maybe more than awful. I tried to push the feeling away and focused on being brave. Sooner or later, we had to run into someone or something and I would need to put my big girl panties on. But for good measure, I stuck close to Geoffrey; I would have bet on him in a fight sooner than the other boys.

Minutes later, we did see something on the horizon—something else besides jungle to our left and ocean to our right. It was still too far away to decipher, but without speaking, we automatically broke into a run. I don't know why, but something drew me—and the rest of my peers—to it. As we neared the object, I could see that it was a large, flat stone supported by other cylindrical stones in the sand. Now, just a few feet away, I noticed the stone was a table of sorts.

The table was on the beach, but far up from the water. There was a bit of a natural inlet in the surrounding plant life that made a crescent shape. The part of the inlet furthest from us rested against low, jagged, brown and purple mountains. The stone was placed inside this crescent, almost sheltered by it. The slab itself was up to Geoffrey's shoulder in height, smooth in texture and charcoal gray in color. There were remnants of dried up, flaky leaves on the surface, as well as leaves that looked freshly picked. I saw stains from what had probably been berries and other fruits. The strangest thing I noticed about the table was cat-like hair that stuck to the dried leaves and evaporated fruit juice. Gross.

Curious, we all examined the stone table, walking around and around. It was simple and primitive. One of the sides had a slanted stone from the top of the table to the sand—a ramp of sorts? It looked like we could walk up the angled surface, but I certainly wasn't in the mood to strut around in dried, crunchy leaves and sticky animal hair.

I touched the cool, round legs of it, wondering what on earth the whole structure could be for. I didn't get to linger in my wonderings because Daniel issued a warning in a high-pitched whisper. "Get over here, you guys! I think someone's coming!"

I felt Geoffrey grab my arm, his fingers digging in hard, and pull me up the beach toward a portion of jungle. He wasn't very gentle and a number of cuss words were running through my head. I was starting to say something, when he glared at me and gave a stern, "Shh!" I swallowed my pride (and my pain) and shut up.

We were all huddled together in a large bush and peeked out of the leaves using our fingers. I still couldn't hear anything and was thinking of some choice words for Daniel too. *He must be crazy and paranoid. I don't hear a dang thing. Maybe he should get his hearing checked...*I was startled by a harsh sound. It was like a cross between a frenzied shriek and a lion's roar, coming from our left, still far off in the distance. Keira make a small yelp sound that was turning into a scream, but Ben quickly cupped his hand over her mouth. Daniel looked at all of us sternly and motioned for us to keep silent by placing his finger over his mouth. We all continued to peer through the bush. I braced myself for the worst, clenching my teeth down with brutal force.

Chapter Seven: Diegen

As the afflicted teenagers awaited their fate that afternoon on the strange beach, they had no idea that their young lives were about to change forever. They were completely unaware there was a being that was the very essence of evil and would do anything to find and kill them. Fortunately for them, he was mostly unaware of their presence on his planet.

He had suspicions that something was amiss but couldn't quite unearth the problem. There had been some rumors circulating that the ancient portal to other worlds had been opened, but even he didn't believe in such fairy tales. Though he was already a person of ill humor, his mood was even fouler as he marched toward his meeting room.

The circular meeting room was well lit by the sunlight cascading in through the multitude of windows strategically placed between the stones in the walls. A high, vaulted ceiling encouraged the light to absorb the entire room.

The light was abundant, but there was a crisp chill in the air, which would bring goose bumps to anyone's skin. In the center of the room, an ancient, rectangular, wooden table with a white lacquered finish filled the space. Half a dozen chairs to match were arranged neatly around it. Strong incense burned in the chamber, which would hit one's nose with an intoxicating, dizzying perfume upon entrance. The thick smell hung in the room as a foreboding shadow, possibly indicating what would soon take place.

But for the table, few chairs and candles, the room was bare. Even the accessories on the table itself were sparse: An old, magic map of all the lands of Cantelia, a small bowl with smoking incense sticks, and an onyx basin with a silver sheen. Sapphire blue liquid filled the basin.

It was deep and fluid but did not reflect any of the surroundings. Instead, it seemed as though it were a deep, bottomless pool in which one could get lost. A metal-studded, white leather door was the only exit. Its silver handle turned quickly, without sound, and three figures entered.

Click-clack, click-clack went the finely polished shoes of one of the figures, breaking the tomb-like silence of the room with their echoes on the stone floor. He too wore white, practically blending in with the room. Leading the other two to the table, he strode forward and seated himself in the tallest, ivory chair.

The one to his left appeared to be a middle-aged man, who had graying wisps of black hair on his head due to an extreme receding hairline. His eyes were a dark brown, almost black color that made him look as though he were continually scheming some horrible plan. Perhaps he was, for he served as the royal advisor.

The figure to the right of the seated man could have passed for human—*if* he wanted. Instead, he proudly wore the mark that most of his kind hid: intricate markings of raised skin on a shaved head, practically shouting what he was and what his capabilities were.

His kind was called the Kotkas. They were one of the worst beings one could run into on Cantelia. Kotkas were a savage, heartless group of human-like creatures that either accepted their role in life as treacherous, master mercenaries or hid what their inner nature desired by trying to live a quiet, peaceful life.

They could live in hiding and cover their marks by growing hair, but if other ruthless Kotkas discovered them, their lives were forfeit. This particular Kotka, who embraced every fiber of his genetic make-up and savage desires, was the best of his kind in the worst way and now he turned to face the royal advisor. A conversation that had begun earlier resumed.

"But my Lord," exclaimed the one to his left, "how can we be certain the...*disturbance* has anything to do with that...that *Prophecy?*" He spat out the last word with utter contempt and disgust.

Feast Island

Diegen rested his limbs on the armrests of his chair and began to curl his pale fingers around their edges. A motion like this usually signaled displeasure and irritation, though to a greater degree than the emotions of anyone else. Today, he was especially agitated because he *knew* there was something amiss in his kingdom but had yet to discover its origins and whereabouts. Nothing yet was displayed on the map but he *knew* there was something out there that he wanted to harbor control over. Whether it was a threat to his kingdom and ultimately his life was to be determined.

As he tightened his grip, his fingers seemed to extend from their natural length and became more bony, jagged and translucent. They looked nearly crippled and fragile, with the exception of the almost visible power that flowed from his fingernails. Shadows from his hood clouded his face, but his eyes became pools of tar. Indeed, his blue eyes were now slowly being overcome by the black color from his pupils. The whites of his eyes disappeared until there was only the glossy darkness, which had an animal-like appearance. He released his grip on the armrests with both hands and slowly pushed back his hood.

Evil often appears as a beautiful light before it entangles and crushes the soul, and Diegen was no exception to that rule—especially because he was evil incarnate itself. Although his eyes had the power and capacity to paralyze anyone with fear, there was a deadness to them, making them appear to be ornate and rare gems. One would probably describe his face as plain, but there was a type of hovering blur to them. There were no sharp angles, no truly defined features. There were no imperfections either. It was as if he could mold and shape his face at will—as if he could make one see what *he* wanted them to see: beauty rather than darkness, serenity rather than absolute hostility.

His gaze slowly took in the lackey on his left. The slight squint of his eyelids was the sole indication of his anger, the rest of his face neatly arranged into a diplomatic and seemingly peaceful countenance.

"Don't test my patience, Propus. You know what I think of the *prophecies*. They are trite and ridiculous fairytales that the Cantelians make up to gain their so-called "hope" that one day they can overthrow my rule—useless, empty words that have no weight. If you mention such things again, I will see to it that your tongue is ripped out so you may never utter an idiotic word again." As Diegen spoke those words, Propus fell to his knees and uttered a sharp cry of agony.

"Please, my Lord! Forgive me!" he screamed. "I will never mention it again! Have mercy! Argh!"

Propus began to feel the pain in his fingertips. Looking down at his nail beds, he witnessed their usual pink color being polluted by a deep red, almost black color: blood, he realized. Once the nail beds completely changed color, they were so pressured by the liquid that they popped off, one by one. The same thing was happening to his toenails, and the close-toed shoes he wore amplified the pain.

As if that was not enough display of power, Diegen continued to concentrate on the inflicted man and soon the veins in Propus's arms and legs were becoming more visible and swollen with blood. It was clear that if his punishment continued, his brain would be the major organ to receive a massive rush of bodily fluid, causing an explosion and his ultimate death. His vision was now muddied and tinted with red, and he fell down, curling into a tight ball, screaming like a child having a nightmare. Unexpectedly, the scorching pain running through his body subsided. He was momentarily paralyzed and whimpered on the floor. Propus moved his eyes slowly and realized he was blind. However, he dared not make another sound.

Diegen began to draw his eyes to his right while rearranging his now dark and grotesque face into a more relaxed, neutral state. His fingers slowly retracted to their usual length and filled out with flesh. Once again, his features were the soft and blurry lines they were before. His eyes changed back to their cold, blue color and the black pupils were as they should be. He looked at the crumpled man with utter contempt.

"Yes, Propus, you are blind," he stated without emotion. "However, I am feeling merciful today so your sight will be restored in a few days. Hopefully this warning will help you remember to keep your unfounded ideas and fantasies to yourself." Then he looked at the creature standing beside the royal advisor.

"And what of your silence, Graffias? Do you have nothing to say about the fairytales?"

"No, my Lord," responded Graffias. Diegen eyed him from head to toe and finally looked back to his advisor, crippled on the ground.

"I tire of your incompetent words, Propus. Graffias escort this idiot out and leave me until I call. I will consult the Vaskur by myself."

Without another word, the Kotka immediately obeyed and easily placed the royal advisor over his broad shoulder. Then he exited the room and the door shut itself, leaving the foreboding man alone with the onyx basin—the Vaskur. After a few moments, Diegen murmured unintelligible words that grew in a crescendo of awful, guttural sounds. The room seemed darker, heavier, and colder than before.

The liquid in the Vaskur started to swirl and red orange dots of color appeared as if coloring had been dropped in. He stared intently at the moving liquid and continued to chant loudly. While the dots formed images, the colors mixed, and black faces with red eyes became visible. One in particular started to speak. "Yes, my Lord?" the creature asked in a gravely voice.

"Ah, Vang...I have some extra...*business* I'd like you to attend to."

Chapter Eight: Feast

More sounds came from our right—rustling sounds. They were becoming louder and obviously nearer as each second ticked away. It was all I could do to keep from screaming. *Great, we're all probably going to die and I've only had one lousy boyfriend who is still a loser.*

I was thinking of the only boy I had ever dated in my short life, Henry Lumpers. Yep. That's his real last name, which should have been reason enough to stay away from him in the first place. Unfortunately I was a little too desperate in junior high and thought that was all I could get. Kissing him had been like making out with a bologna sandwich—mushy and below par. *Bleh!* To my best friend Danielle's relief, I got over it in a few days.

As I tried to make light of our dire situation by revisiting my dating failures—okay, *failure*—I detected movement from the far right part of the thick, greened crescent.

I squeezed my eyes together, as if that would give me super vision, barely breathing. I was soon rubbing my eyes and wiping my glasses, knowing not only that the super vision failed, but that I was probably incapable of seeing straight at all. What emerged from the greenery was a...a wild boar? Seriously?

Yep, it was a wild boar—of sorts. It looked like the ones I had seen in pictures before, but its tusks were rounded and its body was much larger in size. Its face wasn't as boar-like either, appearing to have some human traits in the features. Eyes that showed human intelligence—or was that just my imagination playing tricks on me—were moving from side to side. The fur of the creature was a caramel and cream color, and the hair on its head was long and black.

As I studied it, I was startled as more boars came in a pack, right behind the leading one. They were all carrying makeshift pouches in their mouths, heading right for the stone table. One by one, they trotted up the ramp and placed their pouches down on the surface.

As each pouch fell from a boar's grip, it opened to reveal all types of fruits and nuts and small, dead bird-like kinds of animals. Ew. When they dropped off the food (and dead stuff—again, double ew) they marched back down the ramp and into the portion of jungle from which they came.

I finally noticed that I was starting to drool on myself because, due to shock, my mouth had been open for way too long. Great, now my group would know me as "Alex the Drooler". Perfect. Yet another comforting thought in a potentially dangerous situation. I guess that's what my forte is—knowing how to humiliate myself at every inconvenient moment of my life.

I was momentarily jerked from my thoughts when I heard Geoffrey whisper close to my ear, "Look—more coming." I nearly jumped from the close proximity in such a hazardous moment.

Sure enough, more animals were pouring out of the plant life. But they weren't boars. They were...rats? *What the...?* My eyes grew wide as a procession of mousy-rat animals headed for the same table as the boars had.

They were mean looking, with almost human faces, minus the elongated nose and rough whiskers protruding from their faces of course. Oh...and did I mention they were as tall or taller than myself? Yeah. Creepy-and-a-half. They even had spears.

Their fur was thick and ranged in colors from the black, brown, and gray color families. Their eyes were glossy, black marbles and their tails looked like tattered ropes, beaten to wisps like the ones on an old ship that's seen many storms. So *not* cute. At all. Their nasty feet were hairy and bulbous—kinda like Hobbits. I was so intrigued that I almost forgot how scared I was. Almost.

Some were scurrying on all fours; some walked completely upright. They had lumpy pouches in their hands and mouths. They ascended the table's ramp, dumped out some fruit and ran back down without even looking back. As soon as the rat thingies were no longer in sight, the leaves on the trees near the same spot started to rustle violently and I gasped in horror at the disgusting animals trotting toward the table. Geoffrey reached down to squeeze my hand as a reminder to keep quiet, but his hand lingered in mine for quite some time. It was unexpected.

Had I any food in my stomach, I would have hurled it all out in the bush in front of me. What I saw were feral-looking cats, utterly hairless, with huge warts covering their already wrinkled skin. The only similarity between them and the other animals was again, the human-like features.

Their eyes were bright yellow with green pupils, making them look alien. And well, okay, all the other animals looked alien too, but the cats were over-the-top alien. I caught a good look at the teeth on one of them and shuddered: its set of teeth could have been transplants from a shark for all I knew. I made a mental note to not piss off one of the cats, should I be unlucky enough to encounter one. And the way my luck was going for the day, it would most likely only be a matter of minutes before we were acquainted with said creatures.

Maybe it really *was* the end of the world and these creatures were going to annihilate each and every one of us. Never in my wildest imagination had I pictured such untamed and vicious creatures, all of whom held such cleverness in their eyes. My body felt completely hollow as my heart pounded heavily behind my rib cage. I felt the shocks of my pulse seep down to my toes. Perhaps these symptoms were the beginnings of a panic attack?

The cats followed suit like the other animals and I sincerely hoped they would disappear as quickly as the others so we could leave our hiding spot and run away from that horrible place to find some freaking humans. But alas, my bad luck was stagnant for the day, and I was horribly unsurprised when a few cats lingered about twenty feet south of the table.

Utterly distracted by all the commotion, I failed to notice my right hand now tightly clutching Geoffrey's forearm. I was so embarrassed when he turned to look at me with a questioning expression. I immediately released my grip and mouthed the word, "Sorry", trying to look as penitent as humanly possible.

He surprised me by putting his arm around my shoulder, obviously just as scared—well, maybe—or in the very least anxious, as myself. Totally weird, but I just accepted it. After all, if we made it out of here alive, he would probably dismiss the entire incident. I decided to savor the moment and inched closer to him, expecting only the unexpected. Convincing my imagination to keep from getting the better of me was quite a hard task while feeling his large and muscular arm keeping me grounded. *Geez, I'm so delusional...*But he never retracted or seemed repulsed. Huh.

It was now the second dusk of our day and I wondered what other creepy, unearthly creatures would emerge from the dense jungle. I also began to imagine, due to my ridiculous phobia, what the insects were like if the animals were so awful and menacing. I put my arm around Geoffrey's waist and still, he didn't reject it. A girl could get used to this, minus the alien animals with their dejected fruit and dead creatures. I decided to risk another glance at the cats that were slowly pacing the ground. Beyond them, the dense jungle was darker from lack of sunlight, but I could see glistening dots of bright colors. At first, I thought they were fireflies. I began whispering a question to Geoffrey.

"Do you suppose those little lights are fireflies or something?"

"No", he whispered back. "I think those are the eyes of the other animals waiting."

I should have known. Of *course* they were the eyes of the nasty beasts, not some pretty little bugs. Ugh. I glanced down the line of the others beyond Geoffrey. The other girls seemed even more frightened than myself. They had probably heard my question and it was more than they could handle.

Keira was shaking and Daniel was trying to calm her down by holding her close to his chest. Heather wasn't as bad, but she was definitely freaking out. She gave Geoffrey and me a look of desperation. I held out my free arm to her and she buried her face into my shoulder, quiet sobs beginning to shake her frame. And there I was—"Momma Alex" giving comfort to others as I usually did. I sighed and patted Heather's back. Why did *I* have to pretend to be the brave girl?

I could no longer think about these things because there was a loud roar just then, tearing through the atmosphere and echoing deep into the jungle. The sound of the roar was one of intense hunger. Oh crap. What now? Was this the end for us? We all squeezed tight as a group, too anxious do anything but breathe with caution.

It was just barely light enough to see the sand on the beach being formed into a dust cloud. My vision was weak anyway, succumbed to my stupid glasses. But my hearing was just fine. Fine enough to hear the pounding feet on the sand, quickly approaching the table in a large pack. I expected more freakish-looking animals; instead, I was pleasantly surprised and disturbed at the same time. As soon as the galloping subsided, the animals that appeared when the dust settled were breathtaking—in both a good and bad way.

I wanted to rub my eyes in case they were malfunctioning. Well, okay, I thought they were malfunctioning already by the other sights I had taken in, but this was so different a sight than the others. Glistening in the last remnants of sunlight were horse-sized, bluish black jaguars with sleek coats of fur like liquid silk.

They were extremely stately in posture and stride. I was completely awed by their beauty and mesmerized by everything else they possessed in their build. Their faces also had human-like features and I thought their eyes would be as beautiful as the rest of their bodies.

Instead of gorgeous, captivating eyes, they had blood red, fierce, and menacing eyes. They weren't even glossy; they were flat like a matted finish on a photo. As I looked at them, my whole body became cold and stiff. It was as if I couldn't move, even though my head was screaming *Danger! Danger! Danger!*

These creatures, I felt, were something extremely different than those preceding them. The jaguars, beautiful as they were on the outside, reeked of evil on the inside. I can't describe it any other way. I thought that the others must have had to feel the same way too. There was nothing good that could happen from coming into contact with them. I'm sure one of their paws could have crushed anyone—or anything for that matter—to death.

As they neared the stone table, their gallop slowed to a steady and stealthy stride until they eventually stopped in a military line. There were at least thirty of them, all about the same size and height. In their alignment, they appeared even more fearsome and menacing. There was one who did not join the line, but instead paced back and forth in front of their others. Leader of the pack, perhaps?

The jaguars began to advance at the signal of the one in front. By this time, Heather was shaking like a rattle in a baby's hand and hid behind Geoffrey. Although the whole situation was scary as all hell breaking loose, I was overcome by curiosity and inched forward to get a better view through the leaves.

The assembly of jaguars came closer and closer until they reached the stone table. Most glided up the table's ramp and grotesquely ravaged the food and edibles on the surface. I looked for any trace of the other animals but came across glints of eyes only. However, as my gaze traveled back to the table,

I saw one of the rats standing alone in the chaos of the savage jaguars. It seemed to be taking a fighting stance and had what looked like a spear clutched in its paws...er, hands? Those that had lingered at the base of the table closed the gap between this lone rat and their own pack. I found myself feeling sorry for the mouse, wondering if it would be able to draw out any patience from the hungry beasts. I wasn't betting my life on it.

The creeping jaguars growled deeply, but loud enough to frighten anyone within a mile radius, and I was just yards away. It wasn't like watching The Discovery Channel and hearing a lion roar on a television, and it wasn't even close to being at the zoo. The rodent appeared to be agitating the jaguars—

dumb idea. It hurtled the spear at one of the dark forms but the animal moved too quickly to even receive a scrape.

Immediately, the rest of the pack rushed at the lone rat and began to savagely rip its body apart, without warning or mercy. I was glad the other girls had resorted to squeezing their eyes shut because it was the most horrible sight I had ever witnessed. It was like that cliché phrase people use: "It was like a bad car accident but I couldn't look away."

Though no other rat creatures dared to rush to the aid of their fallen comrade, I could hear angry noises coming from those that were still visible on the beach. The jaguar leader suddenly leapt in front of his savage pack as they finished tearing up their extra meal. He let out a powerful roar—which I thought was either a warning or a preview to something nasty—and those still standing near the stone table began to walk backwards to the thickness of the jungle. The wild, black beast walked with fluidity until it arrived at the point where sand met jungle.

There it stopped, extended its neck to glare at the smaller animals and made a snorting sound. I was almost sure it was going to pounce on them and have a third meal. But, it quickly turned around and began to charge away, his pack following suit. No other animals emerged from the shadows of the foliage and the jaguars were now far away from the table.

Though we knew to keep quiet, just in case, we

Feast Island

all let out sighs of relief and began to turn around to get out of that awful place. As we did, we were met by something even more unexpected: the points of spears belonging to half-naked, ferocious-looking tribesmen. *Boy is this day turning out to be fun.*

Chapter Nine: Tribes

Besides taking a second or two to wonder how we didn't hear the hostile men sneak up on us, I mostly felt a numb compliance to comply with anything they were yelling at us. I just wanted to stay alive long enough to get home for dinner and if that meant I had to give them my social security number and locker combination, I was game. I think that when you start to think things like that in the midst of a dangerous and traumatic situation, it's called "shock". I could barely hear what was being yelled at us. While my brain was slowly trying to process the events of that afternoon, I began to gain my sense of hearing once more.

The men were still pointing their spears at us but now the spears were swinging back and forth, motioning us to come with them. Daniel started to protest and in that instant, the sharp point of a spear was grazing his neck and a small stream of blood began to trickle down.

"Okay, okay..." he said roughly.

With this warning, we all turned in the direction the other spears were pointing to and the sharp point on Daniel's neck slowly lowered. His hand immediately went up to his neck but he didn't make any other sounds or gestures as he followed the leader of the tribal group. We were forced into a single file line, which reminded me of being in elementary school, except my teachers never used weapons to keep us in line—or took us hostage for that matter. Talk about incentive.

As we trudged along, the men were talking in hushed voices in a language I didn't know. The sounds they made were very syncopated and harsh—definitely not a language I was familiar with. While they spoke, I risked whispering to Daniel who was in front of me.

"Daniel how's your neck?"

"I'll live", he whispered grimly.

"Is it still bleeding?"

"A bit, but it should be fine. Thanks."

I didn't inquire further since his answers weren't full of information and because the men quieted their own chatter. We were silent during the rest of our trek through the foreign jungle. With darkness falling, I did my best to take everything in— every sight, every sound, every feeling I was experiencing.

The plants were lush and green and giant. They were certainly larger than any plants I had watched on documentaries of the rainforest. There were also colors that I had never seen in any botanical setting. Some flowers had so many colors that they looked like tie-dyed t-shirts.

The smells all around were strong, sweet, musky and fresh. It was a lot for my nose to take in. I also eyed some round objects growing from the trees and plant vines—objects that I assumed to be fruit. Most of the fruits were the brightest neon colors I had ever laid my eyes upon. So bright, in fact, that they were glowing in the dark, as if they were lit from within.

As fascinating as everything was, I was still scared out of my mind. My imagination could have never made up the sights right in front of my eyes. I mean, here I was in who knew where, with people I barely knew, strangers who were hostile, and other dangerous creatures that could rip my throat out in the blink of an eye. Never mind about being home late for dinner; I wondered if I'd ever make it home again. Since my thoughts weren't very positive, my eyes welled up and silent tears trickled down my cheeks. The only thing I could do was pray that we'd all make it out alive.

I was distracted from my misery by a noise from the back of our line. Poor Heather tripped and made a muffled sound of pain. The men following up the rear of our shuffle instantly pointed their spears toward her fallen body, shouting curses for all I knew. Before I could stop myself, I was shouting, "Stop it! She's not going to do anything!"

That was not a good idea because the men in

the front were now pointing spears and yelling at me too. One of them licked his lips—what a pig. Now the tears that silently snaked down my face turned into a blubbering waterfall. I froze from fear.

But when the sharp tips of promising nothing but violence were inches from my head, a loud and commanding voice echoed through the jungle. I don't know what it said, but it made the savages—yes, I had now upgraded them to savages in my mind—lower their weapons and back the heck away. *Thank goodness.*

Though extremely relieved, I don't think any in our group were foolish enough to let our guard down. Heather was still crumpled on the ground and Ben cautiously lowered his body to help pull her up. Physically she looked fine, but her face was a wretch of nerves. *"Sorry,"* she barely managed to mouth to the rest of us.

In those fleeting seconds, the owner of the loud voice appeared as if by a switch. He was a few inches taller than the savages who were still surrounding us. His skin was as tanned as any typical tropical dweller would be, and he had a slightly protruding belly (guess he didn't hunt as much anymore). He rocked one of the strangest haircuts I'd ever seen with braids and patches of a buzz cut. Beady brown eyes were set in a serious, weathered face that had probably seen years and years of hardships. This man was definitely chief material.

His dark eyes were now set on Daniel, who was the tallest in our crew, which I guess made him the leader. The guttural, incomprehensible sounds that the savages had gushed out before were coming from the man's mouth and it looked like he wanted an explanation from Daniel. He wasn't hostile but you got the feeling that he was a man of one chance, and one chance only.

Daniel, I'm sure, wanted to turn and run but you'd never know it by looking at how he stood there, calm and collected. His voice was a bit shaky, but confident as he began to formulate a response.

"I'm sorry sir, but I don't understand what you're saying," he began slowly. "My name is Daniel and these are my friends. We don't know how we got here, but we mean no harm. We come in peace."

He raised both hands up, palms toward his interrogator, in a gesture of innocence. *We come in peace? Really? How cliché can you get?* Our eyes were now on the tall man and I held my breath in anticipation. *Please, oh please let him have mercy on us!* His eyes looked puzzled and then grew wide. I couldn't yet tell if this was a good thing or a bad thing. His eyes, nose and mouth then squeezed together for a second and relaxed. He started laughing. *What the crap?*

Once the laughter died down, his countenance was softer and he spoke again. We were all startled and surprised when we could understand the sounds he was making.

"I...am Kodu," he said with a very thick accent. He was pointing with his thumb to his chest. "Come, we go my village and I tell everything." Only, "everything" sounded like *evee-teeng.* And who said miracles don't happen anymore? The man, whom now I really assumed was the chief of these crazy people, spoke English. *Well that's unexpected...*

He yelled in his own language to the minions and though they stayed close, they kept their weaponry low and looked at us with shameless curiosity, a welcome break from looks of *I-might-eat-you-for-dinner-if-I-become-hungry-enough.*

For our own posterity, we stayed in a single file formation and followed our surprise redeemer. Daniel still led the line and I managed to remain second. I figured that being closer to the chief and to Daniel, our assumed chief, would perhaps extend my life expectancy.

Kodu's wrinkles made him look like he was a great-grandfather, yet he walked with the energy of an eight-year-old. He was agile, sprightly and fully aware of his surroundings. Hopefully he meant to remain on our side because though he sported a semi-potbelly, I knew he was just as much of a warrior now as he probably was decades before.

Wherever we were going, I wished that we would arrive soon. I was starving, tired and too irritated to be scared anymore. I wondered what information he had that would interest us in any way, unless it had to do with giving directions for making it back home. Maybe it was like we all feared—that the world was coming to an end by some series of insane and unreal events and we were blasted by nuclear warfare to a remote island where we would be forced to live out the rest of our days in loincloths and leaf tops until facing death from radiation poisoning. Okay, well at least that's what *I* feared.

After what felt like days but was actually about twenty minutes, a strong but inviting smell of roasted meat filled my senses and pulled me out of my daydreaming. "Thank God!" Keira exploded. "There's actually food and shelter!"

I peered around Daniel's broad shoulders and witnessed what she had: a grouping of tribal huts was nestled in a clearing and in the middle of the settlement was a huge fire pit with several animals roasting on a very long spit.

Women were tending to the food—they seemed to have clothes covering the important parts (thank God)—and kids about our age were performing a variety of tasks: sharpening weaponry, braiding plant vines together to make baskets and containers, playing games with younger children. It was like a snapshot out of National Geographic magazine. When the busy people became aware of our group, they froze in their chatter and activities and stared.

Chief Kodu made a shouting announcement as

the rest of the group entered the clearing. Heather limped carefully to my side and put her arm through mine. We waited for the chief to finish his broadcast and while we did so, I kept thinking *I hope he's not telling them to add us to those spits for dinner.* Finally, he turned to us and the whole village was stirring once more. Some began to voice eerie chants and scurried to take the meat down from the fire.

"Before we talk, we eat," he said with his thick accent. "We are honored to have the Chosen Ones on our island." He smiled, revealing a three-toothed smile. My dentist would have been horrified. Heck, I was horrified.

Daniel spoke for us. "*Chosen Ones?* What do you mean sir? I'm sorry, but you have us mistaken with some other group I'm sure."

"I make no mistake," the chief replied harshly. "Now we eat. Come."

Though we were all baffled by our given group title and exchanged looks of perplexity, not a one of us refused to follow him since there was the promise of dinner in our immediate future. Just thinking about a hot meal hitting my empty stomach was all the motivation I mustered my last reserves of adrenaline and march with the others to a seating area.

By now, darkness had fallen and some of the women were busy lighting torches that sat on the outskirts of the small village. Everything was still foreign but the lights in the darkness gave off a cheery and homey feeling.

In front of the largest hut, there were grass mats placed in casual groupings but I knew our group would be the most prominent. After all, we were sitting with the chief himself. He pointed to the mats, indicating that we were to sit and we nearly landed on each other while collapsing on our rears. Finally, relief came to my tired feet.

We sat in an incomplete circle, so maybe others of importance in the tribe would join us soon. Geoffrey was to my left and Heather was on my right. Next to Geoffrey were Justin and Daniel. Next to Heather were Keira and Ben. Our backs were facing the large hut so we had a solid view of the fire and giant spit.

Most of the villagers were quickly dividing the meat into portions on large plant leaves. The warriors who had escorted us through the jungle had already found their own groups to eat with and were being waited on. Some young children approached us cautiously and set down roughly-made wooden cups and a young girl—maybe about eleven—followed closely behind them and began to pour a rich brown liquid from what appeared to be an old animal skin.

I had seen pictures of liquid-holding animal skins before in museums but never before in real life. I tried not to become nauseated from thinking about all the germs that could possibly be floating around in the container.

Though I was only fourteen, I knew better than

to protest or refuse their hospitality. The key to staying alive in savage places was to be agreeable and I sure hoped everyone else was on board with my way of thinking. If Keira fussed, I was ready to punch her in the mouth. Heather had been talking to me but I had just now noticed.

"Sorry, what did you say Heather?" I frowned.

"Oh, I was just asking if you thought they have Purell. My hands are disgusting, but I'm guessing I'll just have to deal with it."

I tried to keep a straight face. *Purell in the JUNGLE?! Oh this silly girl...*

"Yeah, you're gonna have to deal with it. Sorry. I highly doubt that they even know what the word *sanitize* means. Just try not to think about it, okay? Maybe we can find some water to wash with later."

After the young girl left us, another group walked toward us. This time, it was a cluster of women of varying ages: some old, some young, some in between. They all had an unreal energy about them however, and were beautiful in their own way. Even those with wrinkles were attractive and gave off an air of regal kindness and warmth.

While watching them, I began to wonder whether the "Fountain of Youth" really did exist and if it was housed in their midst. Or possibly there were healing or preserving powers in their food—the glowing fruit I had seen earlier perhaps?

The women placed a large plant leaf filled with

steaming meat in front of each of us. The chief was still standing close, barking orders, pointing everywhere, and watching our reactions with interest. I was so glad that bugs weren't on the menu...yet. If my food started wiggling, I would pass out right then and there.

Daniel's eyes grew wide with pleasure as the meaty aroma hit his senses. He started to pick up a piece of meat but Ben made a throat clearing sound. Daniel froze midair and looked at him. Ben violently shook his head and motioned to Kodu who was now talking to a young man. Daniel scowled but obediently set his food back down and avoided eye contact with the rest of us. Justin chuckled quietly. And I thought *I* was a bear when starving.

Finally the chief stopped talking to the young man and raised both hands in the air. Everyone fell silent in an instant and eagerly waited for the next words of their leader to be spoken. There was such devotion and respect emanating from every single person.

I half expected him to roar like a lion, and he practically did. Well, he didn't *really* but that's what their language sounded like. As he projected his voice, he pointed to us and made gestures with his hand. All the people stared at us for the millionth time and slowly nodded as the chief continued. Finally, he paused, and when my mouth was salivating heavily I jolted from the surprise of a booming battle cry. The tribe echoed his yell and then turned to their groups

Feast Island

and commenced with dinner.

"Now we eat," Chief Kodu exclaimed as he sat down with crossed legs. I was extremely grateful that his loincloth covered all the things I didn't want to see during dinner or *ever*. Some older men came to join our circle and sat by him. They chattered in a hurried manner, like old gossips. It was like hearing clucking and cooing chickens. Most had long, white braids as hairstyles. Some carried canes or intricately carved walking sticks and set them down after sitting on the mats.

As they spoke and ate, they continually stared at us. I felt like I was part of some zoo. To distract myself, I decided to make small talk with Geoffrey. I sincerely hoped it would go better than the mean glare he had given me only that afternoon—and afternoon that seemed to have dragged on for quite some time.

"So..." I began. "Thanks for helping me to freak out a little less than normal on the beach today. I really appreciated that." He looked at me with an expression that said, *Are you talking to me?* All I could do was raise my eyebrows and exert my head forward a bit. "So yeah, thanks. That's all." I didn't expect anything, but hey, at least I made an effort.

"You're welcome," he replied quietly, after a few moments. *Maybe the Grinch has a heart!*

"Some day, huh?" It was the only brilliant thing I could think of to continue the already awkward conversation. "I mean...who would have thought we'd

have such an adventure just to film a stupid project?"
Again, the drawn out, painful silence. But he
responded with a few more words than before.

"Yeah. I think we're all kinda in shock. I don't
know what's going on, but we better figure out how to
get out of here as soon as we can." And he left it at
that. Heather was a better conservationist, so I decided
to turn to her instead and leave the awkwardness with
Geoffrey. But when I turned to face Heather,
something—or rather, *someone*—caught my eye like a
favorite candy.

The young man whom Kodu had spoken with
earlier approached our gathering. He held a leaf of
piled meat in one hand and an extra mat in the other.
He floated the mat down right between Keira and
Heather and managed to gracefully fold into a sitting
position while grinning at Keira. All I could see of him
was his straight, shoulder-length locks and toned and
tanned left arm. To my surprise, she actually smiled at
him. He turned to face Heather and that's when I got a
really good look at his face. He was very handsome and
I felt the tugs of a smile on my mouth.

His lips, his *perfect* lips, were just as pouty and
full as Keira's. His chin had a small dimple in it, only
adding to the masculinity of his square-set jawbones.
His nose could have been featured as a prototype for
rhinoplasty and high cheekbones framed it effortlessly.

His forehead was smooth and just the right
distance from his black, thick—but not *too* thick—

eyebrows and hairline. Finally, the eyes...his eyes...were shaped like almonds with a sphere of dark chocolate in each. Those eyes almost made me forget that I was very hungry and now I was in a full grin.

I guessed him to be anywhere from eighteen to twenty-one. He actually leaned over Heather, engaging the carved muscles in his torso and looked my way. All my dreams of getting lost in his eyes were quickly crushed when he said, "What is that?" in accented, but clear English. He was pointing to my teeth.

I released my stupid smile and responded in a dull voice, "My braces."

"What is...bray-sezz?" he asked. I sighed and before I could explain, Keira answered for me in her own way.

"Oh, don't worry about her," she smirked as she placed her hand on his forearm. "Those are just hideous pieces of metal glued to her horse teeth. Nothing special there."

"You once had braces too, *Miss Perfect!*" I sneered. "And if you continue to be a jerk, I'll punch your pretty little face and knock out a few of those perfectly placed teeth." I hated how my temper had reared its ugly head but I wasn't sorry one bit for my reaction. I legitimately wanted to punch her in the face. Keira's shocked expression turned to anger as she began to launch towards me, but the tribal hunk stopped her.

"Stop this!" he commanded. "If you are to help

us, you must not fight each other."

I blushed and looked away; Pouty Princess simply made a *humph* sound and turned to her dinner. The boys had witnessed the hostile exchange and I was too angry to be embarrassed. Geoffrey was quietly chuckling. I don't think I'd ever heard him laugh since we met at the beginning of the school year.

"What do you mean, 'Help us?'" Heather asked the young man sitting next to her.

"Chief Kodu, he will tell you everything when we finish here. For now, please enjoy your food. I sat here to learn more about you—all of you," he finished, looking each one of us square in the eye.

"What's your name?" asked Daniel.

Smiling with slightly crooked, but very white teeth, he slapped his palm to his chest. "I am Kumani. My father, Falu, is brother to Kodu." He motioned to a man sitting to Kodu's right. "Our people have lived on the island for many, many suns, even before the demon lord ruled over us. We have fought in many battles. Now we face an enemy we cannot kill and we lost many great warriors." He paused, seeming to be careful about his next bit of information. "The chief's son, Kosan, the Evil Ones killed him today." He frowned as he finished the last sentence.

"Sorry to hear that. It must be hard for the chief to lose his son. Not to be insensitive and change the subject, but where did you learn to speak English?" questioned Ben.

Kumani looked confused for a split second and then answered, "From the Brotherhood." He stated it matter-of-factly, as if that simple statement should have answered all our questions.

"The *who*?" I blurted.

"You mean you do not know the Brotherhood?" He sounded appalled.

"Well, if you haven't noticed, we're not from around here," Geoffrey stated the obvious.

"I know this, young one," he started to say. I scowled when he called me *young one* and decided that I didn't like him anymore. "But," he continued, "I believed that since they called for you, you would know them."

"Oh," was the only thing I could think of to say.

"Can you please tell us who or what the Brotherhood is?" asked Ben. "Does this have to do with why the chief called us 'Chosen Ones?'"

Kumani quickly looked in the direction of the chief and then back to our anticipated expressions. He opened his mouth but then seemed to rapidly change his mind and closed it. We were still waiting and after a minute, I couldn't take it anymore.

"Well?" I knew I sounded exasperated but didn't care.

"I think it best to learn about the Brotherhood from Kodu. He may be angry if I say too much. Please, finish your meal and then he will take you to our meeting place to explain," he urged.

Though we all made frustrated grunts, he would not be swayed to give further information so we finished dinner in silence. Kumani and Keira seemed to make small talk here and there, but even she wasn't her usual chatterbox self. The meat we ate was very tasty but could have stood to have some salt added.

Having a full stomach and feeling the heat from the blazing fire in the middle of the village made me sleepy. My eyes were droopy and my head was suddenly very heavy. I knew there was much to discuss and find answers to, but I felt so warm and safe. The next thing I knew, Geoffrey was gently shaking me awake. I had fallen asleep on his shoulder for only a few minutes. "Sorry," I mumbled. "Guess I was really tired."

"It is okay," he said gently. "Come; it is time to talk to Chief Kodu."

Feast Island

Chapter Ten: The Prophecy and the Problem

I thought the whole village would be squeezed into the main meeting hut, but apparently only the VIPs were welcome. And by VIPs, I mean all the men who were older than the lot of us. No women, no children; just guys in loincloths and our teenaged group of seven. Kumani stood very near to us but it brought no comfort to me. It appeared that he was the youngest tribesman allowed in the special meeting. Being the nephew of the chief definitely has its perks. Before we had gathered in the hut, we quickly nominated and voted Daniel as our spokesperson. Here's hoping our choice was wise.

Kodu sat at the head of the building on a raised platform, legs crossed and back straight as the path of a saint. His brother, Falu, was sitting at his right and a very old, white-haired man sat to the left. The old man secured a wooden, carved and crooked walking stick across his lap. It was very serpentine in shape and size. There were other men of varying ages standing behind them, the rest of the crowd standing along the sides of the dried grass walls. Loud and constant chatter reverberated around us until the old man at the front raised his stick in the air Moses-style.

At once, silence filled the room and all regressed to their new favorite pastime: staring at us. Heather loomed so close to me that we were almost touching. The boys semi-surrounded us girls while Daniel stood at the front of our formation. Geoffrey had chosen to stand right behind me. The chief uttered something in the tribal tongue while looking at the faces in the hut. When he finished, some men began to whisper to one another and point accusatory fingers at us. All the attention was wearing on me and I longed for sleep. Kodu finally spoke in English.

"Chosen Ones," he began, causing me to roll my eyes. "We think you here to save us from evil curse of Dark One. Ata (here he gestured to the ancient man to his left) say you are Chosen Ones from what was written long, long ago." *Huh?* Baffled by this explanation, we looked to Daniel to say something and clear up all the talk of nonsense and superstition.

"Chief Kodu, you keep calling us Chosen Ones," Daniel said earnestly. "And from what I understood, you said that there is some kind of force on this island—something evil—that has everyone cursed. Well, with all due respect, we're just kids. How is it that you've come to think we can help you with your problems? Aren't there others who can help you? We're just lost from some freak accident and we'd really like to go home soon."

We all nodded in agreement. Finally, someone had said something intelligent. Before Kodu could respond, Kumani walked forward in a humble manner and very softly spoke something to his uncle. The impatient look growing on the chief's face dissipated and he looked thoughtful. He then nodded and Kumani turned to face our group.

"I have asked the chief permission to speak further on his words but I need to ask you something first. You continue to say that you want to go home, but where is home?" He clearly did not intend to say more until we answered his question.

"We're from Pollock Pines, California," replied Daniel, certain that this would be a sufficient answer. Now it was Kumani's turn to look baffled but his reply completely blew me out of the water.

"What planet is that?" *Say...WHAT?*

"Planet?" Daniel said. "*Planet?* Why, Earth, of course. The planet we're on now." I was afraid to hear more but prepared my ears for what my intuition was expecting to find out.

"We are not on Earth, but I have heard of your planet before." Kumani spoke casually as if we were hanging out at a coffee shop. Keira couldn't contain her composure or silence anymore.

"What do you *mean* we're *not* on Earth? This is not a time to be funny. We seriously want to go home. If we need to buy plane or train tickets or something, I'll just find a place to call my dad and he'll wire us the money and then we'll—" But she got no further, for the room busted into chatter.

Kumani was shaking his head, Kodu was trying to gain control of all the erupted conversation and of course, the group of us was nearly in hysterics. Even calm and usually cool Ben was beside himself and for once didn't have an answer. It was too much to take in at once. I felt an asthma attack coming on but tried to slow down my breathing and hold back the threat of tears. Once again, the ancient, white-haired man raised his walking stick and the room hushed. Kumani spoke.

"Your money is no good here Keira. Yes, you are on a different planet—not Earth. You speak of leaving by ways I do not know, but I believe it is what we call false magic. You have come here by true magic because you are needed. Only true magic can take you home, back to your planet."

"So where are we then?" asked Ben. I guessed he didn't want to wait for Daniel to ask all the questions and Daniel seemed indifferent anyway.

"You are in the land called, in the common tongue, 'Land Of Song'. In your language, I believe you would say 'Cantelia'. The planet we are on has no name you would understand in your tongue, but our light—what I think you call 'sun' on your planet—is the star we call *Elnaleth,* which sits on the right horn of the Great Bull in the sky.

"There is also another star close by which does

not give our world as much light as the great one. This place," here, he motioned all around us with his arms, "is our home—Sikuku." He paused—perhaps for dramatic effect—and I saw Justin whispering something to Daniel. Kumani noticed and asked Daniel, "Does your friend have something to say?"

"Yes, he does," replied Daniel. But instead of addressing Kumani, he looked directly at the chief and said, "Chief, can my brother have permission to speak? He thinks he knows something."

All that the chief did for a response was nod, so Daniel nudged a nervous looking Justin. At first, I thought he was going to chicken out, but Justin somehow mustered the nerve to speak up. He stepped slightly forward from our misshapen circle and enlightened us all with his extensive knowledge of celestial bodies.

"I think I know where we are," he began slowly. He was speaking to us more than anyone else, but those who understood English seemed intrigued. "If I am hearing Kumani correctly," he continued, "then I think we're in the Taurus constellation. The star that is the sun on this planet sits on the horn of the bull and is one of the brightest stars in the galaxy. The constellation is sort of on the edge of our galaxy too and this bright star has another star nearby so it's binary.

"I don't know that scientists have identified planets around the star, but it is very possible since there's a ton of galactic material surrounding it." He stopped for a bit to consider his next words.

"I always *knew* there were other life forms out there but I didn't want to get my hopes up. However we got here, it's really amazing—something that humans aren't capable of yet with space travel."

It was the most I had ever heard Justin speak in one sitting. Though frightened, tired, and losing my sanity, I was also intrigued by the information he had given. It was barely beginning to sink in that we were far from home—like, really, *really* far from home.

I knew I wasn't dreaming because even my wild imagination could never have come up with the events that had taken place since crawling onto a foreign beach that afternoon. We needed a plan of action and the right resources to get us back home. For a minute, I wondered if they had any type of sedative in this depraved and creepy jungle. I'd need one to get some good sleep.

Something that bothered me about what Justin had said though, was the apparent excitement in his tone. I just couldn't comprehend why anyone would be excited to find that they've been magically transported to another planet. We obviously had different ambitions in life. Ben's voice brought me back to consciousness.

"Excuse me for speaking out of turn chief," he began, addressing Kodu, "but is it really true? We're on a different planet—not Earth?"

"Yes," he replied. "This why I say you *Chosen*

Ones. We have writing that you come from very far away place. There evil that happen on this island. The black cats—they very bad and try to kill us if we do not bring food everyday. They were tribe of Vang, but the Evil One, he kill all women of tribe and curse the men of Vang. Vang try to rule us by killing my people. We need help to stop curse. This also why I bring you to meeting place—to tell you of old, very old, writings."

When he finished speaking, he looked at his nephew and spoke in the tribal tongue once more. Kumani approached the very ancient, wrinkled man who was still sitting cross-legged with his walking stick across his lap. He bent down on one knee, lowered his head and offered his right hand, palm up. The motions were very ritualistic. I had no idea what he could possibly be getting ready for. Did I want to find out?

The old man began to twist the large stick in his hands and he pulled the top off, revealing a secret compartment of sorts. From it, he pulled out a dark, thick parchment type of document—possibly some kind of tree bark—and gently handed it to Kumani. He turned to face the rest of the room and addressed us.

"Because you do not know about the ancient writings—the uh...prof...profee..." he seemed lost in his words. I couldn't just stand there and let the moment become awkward so I offered a word I thought would help. "Prophecy?"

"Yes. Thank you," he replied, slightly inclining

his head towards me.

"That is what you call it in your tongue. Please forgive me; I have learned your tongue as a boy but have not spoken it often. There is a group that all peoples on this planet look to for hope. They are called the Brotherhood and they keep this prophecy for all people. They pass it on to as many as will receive it so they can keep it safe within their villages, tribes, families—all those who long for the end of these evil days. The Brotherhood has taught many how to speak in your tongue to prepare for your arrival. As I began to say, because it appears you do not know about the ancient writings, the chief has asked me to read it to you:

'One day to come
A time to be
Destruction for some
The rest will be free
Our land of song
Shall be singing again
Broken dreams so long
New lives we'll begin
While we wait we hope
That all evil will cease
It helps us to cope
Until the alien six bring our peace'"

As he looked up from the crude scroll, Geoffrey

snorted in mockery.

"Do you really believe all this crap? It sounds like a stupid fairytale written to let the government get away with its acts of injustice. At least, injustice according to you guys. Besides, there're *seven* of us anyway—not six—and it's not like all of us have the capacity to fight even one person—believe me, I know what I'm talking about. Some of our group—take offense if you want," he raised his eyebrows at us, "couldn't last thirty seconds in a real fight. I have to agree with the guys as I repeat what we've all told you: you have the wrong people."

He folded his arms across his chest, his body in a defiant stance. Without warning, the withered old man stood in one, slick motion, pointed the stick at us and shouted in the awful sounding language of the tribe. It was obvious that he was heated. Once he stopped the yelling fest, the chief addressed us specifically.

"You make Ata very angry, young ones. He say he *know* you are Chosen Ones. He has lived very long and see many, many things. He also know magic and he say you have magic in you. You come from stars." Heather giggled, Justin nodded eagerly, and Geoffrey rolled his eyes. "He say it, we believe it."

In other words, he meant, Ata says what goes and now you have to deal with it. I couldn't translate their weird language, but I had become pretty good at translating underlying meanings, especially with an older sister in the house. We all stood there and tried to soak in everything. I spotted Kodu nodding at Kumani. Looked like we would have to hear the obnoxious tribal hunk speak yet again.

"There is one more thing," he started to say slowly. "We have a problem in our tribe that needs your help right away. The daughter of the chief, Resina, has been taken from us just three days ago. She was to become the wife of the son of the chief of another tribe. His name is Akeen. He claims he does not know where she is, but we believe he does.

"We think he took her away and wants our tribe to be weak because now we have to look for her *and* gather food each day. The other tribe on this island does not trust our tribe or the tribe of Akeen and they will kill us if we go into their part of the island. They do not help us.

"Many years ago, all three tribes were friends and could fight any enemy together; now we all hate one another and there is no more balance on the island for any. We thought we could have peace through the love of Akeen and Resina, but when Resina was not found, the peace ended. Something must be done so we can destroy the dark and evil cats and the rest of our enemies. Can you help us?"

Before any one of us could protest or say otherwise, Kodu stood up and said, "It is spoken. Now we go to sleep. Tomorrow night we talk more. The warriors take you to huts."

Feast Island

At once, we were escorted from the meeting hut with warriors flanked on both sides while the other tribesmen exited the structure, chatting animatedly. It felt like a prisoners' march. The rest of the tribe members had turned in for the night and the only sounds were our marching feet, the crackling of the torches lining the outskirts of the furthest huts, and crickets...at least, I *hoped* the loud, melodic chirps were crickets.

We didn't try to speak to one another, but I think we all knew that the situation was getting out of hand. A cluster of small huts was coming into view and I decided to let my traumatized thoughts have a rest until tomorrow morning. My heavy sigh was interrupted by Daniel's voice.

"Wait a minute, why are you pointing spears at us again? Didn't you hear the chief? We're the *Chosen Ones*."

His last phrase would have been comical, especially since he used a sarcastic undertone, but I didn't find the sharp tips of spears pointing towards the boys very funny. The men surrounding the boys were using the weapons as directional tools, but their tone of voice and facial expressions appeared hostile.

I never thought I would have felt this, but I was actually thankful to see Kumani run up to us and say something to our guards. They lowered their spears when he spoke to them, but they unfortunately lingered.

Keira, in a voice I assumed she thought was seductive but sounded very whiney, asked, "Kumani, what's the problem?" It was too dark for him to notice her batting her eyelashes in his direction.

He flashed a very broad grin at her and replied, "The warriors were told to keep you young women and the young men in different huts. They thought if they used their weapons against the boys, the boys would go to their hut and you would go to yours. I think they do not think well of your friends." He ended his explanation with a little smirk on his face.

I didn't think very well of him and had enough. My stomach had begun to feel a bit sour and I simply wanted to stop moving around everywhere and facing something disturbing at every angle. Perhaps the meat from our dinner hadn't been fully cooked or otherwise. I needed sleep and I needed it now.

"Can you please ask them to just let us go in our huts and sleep? We promise we'll go to the right places." I tried to keep some patience in my inflections but it was becoming harder by the minute. At least he complied by directing the men to stand aside. He told the boys to go into the hut to our left and that there were grass mats waiting for them on the floor.

As he led us a few feet away to the right, I noticed two guards were posted at the entrance of the boys' resting place. Great. That definitely meant we were more prisoner status than "Chosen Ones" status. It also meant that the two men following behind us were probably going to post themselves at our front door.

Kumani opened the patched and worn door for us, holding a torch high to give us light as we entered. There were simply three straw-colored mats side by side on the leaf-covered floor. Three narrow, high-placed windows adorned the walls and the moonlight and starlight shone brightly through them. A small, woven basket of sorts sat in the left most corner. *I guess that would be the bathroom—ugh.* Heather and I entered right behind one another while Keira lingered at the door.

"Thanks for everything Kumani," she said sweetly. "See you in the morning?"

"No, we will meet again at dark. We must hunt and gather tribute during the day. Sleep as long as you want and call one of the guards if you need something."

Before any could reply, he bowed and left swiftly. The guards quickly closed the door and Keira turned around to face Heather and I, a look of dejection on her face. I didn't feel bad for her though; I just wanted to sleep. Besides, my stomach was still not feeling very well and I lacked empathy. Suddenly, I felt the urge to throw up. Color and warmth were rapidly draining from my face and I grabbed the basket to contain the mess that would soon surface.

"Alex, you okay?" asked Heather.

"Ew! She's gonna hurl!" Keira didn't hide how appalled she was. I would have slapped her if both my hands hadn't been occupied. At least Heather cared. She came over to help me hold the bucket and rub small circles on my back.

"Just let it out," she cooed in a comforting manner.

After a few horrible episodes of projectile vomiting, I was able to get words out. "I think I have food poisoning," I said weakly. "This is awful—" But I couldn't say anything after that; another round was ready to be fired.

Out of nowhere, my vision blurred and I started to see spots. The spots were floating around and changing to different colors. This made me feel even worse. Then, unexpected and immense relief washed over me. I felt lighter and no longer weighed down by my sour stomach. It was all very strange; one minute I was bowled over in pain, feeling like...well, *you know*, and then the next I was great.

Tired of staring at the basket, I lifted my head up to tell Heather that by some miracle, I was better. But when I spoke, she was still looking down in concern without acknowledging me at all. She looked like she was talking to herself and I could barely make out what she was saying. I tried to get her attention again, however, she didn't budge. Finally, I decided to get up and that's when I freaked out. When I stood, I was standing in the middle of someone's body—*my* body. At first, I thought I died but then I realized that my poor other self (or whatever) was still moving and throwing up, having an absolutely miserable night. Keira was on the opposite end of the hut with a grimace on her face. She seemed to be saying something to Heather but it was barely audible.

All the loud, grotesque sounds of the prior minutes were nearly muted like when you go to a rock concert and can barely hear what your friends are saying after the show because your ears are still ringing. I risked moving, finding myself eerily transparent, and walked right through my physical body and part of Heather's arm. As if my day hadn't been weird enough, this was the cherry on top—or perhaps the sprinkles. The chocolate kind, of course.

I don't know what compelled me, but I knew I had to leave the hut right then and there. Something important was out there and I had to find it. I looked down again at myself and frowned. Hopefully I could sleep off the sickness and be okay by morning. Heather would take care of me. Keira was just an absolute prick so I didn't waste time worrying about her. I did, however, walk right through her and could have sworn she shivered slightly. It made me smile.

The beginnings of dense jungle were just a few feet away and I walked through the wall of our hut with ease. Though my stomach pains were gone, I couldn't shake a sense of foreboding in my gut—that something was approaching and it was vital to escape. With only my intuition to guide me, I rolled with it and broke into a sprint to face whatever lay ahead.

Chapter Eleven: Explanation and Escape

I ran quickly through the dense jungle, a feeling of urgency steadily building. It was nice to not be out of breath for once. I was running from something but couldn't figure out exactly what. Whatever the thing or presence, I knew it to be dangerous and didn't want to let it cross my path—even though I wasn't in my physical body. The trees, vines and plants seemed endless and my hope of escape dissipated.

My gut told me to take a left turn at the next clearing (a slight clearing, if anything) so I did. To my relief, the beach appeared just yards away and a small cave sat cozy in the jagged cliff that jutted out into the sparkling ocean. The water looked inviting with its small waves and warm temperature and I felt an urge to swim through it to reach the cave. I *had* to get to that cave because it would be safe there. At least, that's what my gut told me.

When I reached a small landing leading up to the mouth of the cave, a hand reached out to pull me to solid ground. The hand was warm and strong and it didn't seem weird to grab it and receive help. It did seem weird that it was solid to me, being that my body was far off in a hut.

As I stood, my hooded helper already had his or her back turned from me while walking slowly to the cave. I simply followed the stranger without question. An unspoken command to do so reverberated in every cell of my body. It was strange to be experiencing this out of body phenomenon and be able to feel what I was feeling. However, as it was my first time in this state, I had nothing to compare it to.

Inside the natural shelter, my companion turned to face me. The man had a smooth, hairless head, murky brown eyes that drooped slightly but looked kind, and features that could have identified him as "any man". There were some small scars on his face—the kind that fights and such bring—and he dressed simply. He wore a brown cape of sorts, a white linen top and loose-fitting brown pants with soft, black leather boots. I half expected to see a sword at his side but there wasn't. Though his clothes were kind of old school, he could have fit in anywhere—into any place or time.

The only thing that was out of place in his get up was a small scar on his neck from a branding tool. It was shaped like a crescent moon with two horizontal lines and a slanted, vertical slash going through it. Who knows how I figured that part out; clearly he had a purpose for finding me and somehow learning about the purpose would be crucial to my survival on this crazy island and strange planet. This all should have freaked me out, but I was too at ease to be frightened. Somehow I knew he would speak first, so I simply waited.

He motioned for me to be seated so I sat down cross-legged on the cool, damp rock. Squatting near me, he outstretched his arms with his hands side-by-side, palm down. After moving them in a circular motion, a blazing campfire popped out of nowhere. I moved closer to the warmth, reaching my hands out to the flames that were now dancing happily. Now that I felt comfortable, my curiosity hit me like a bullet and I tried to peer discreetly at my companion.

He must have felt my eyes upon him because at that moment, he looked up from the fire and removed his hood. His eyes were so reflective and incredibly light that they mimicked prisms. He had goatee-styled facial hair. The only remarkable thing about him was his eye color. It was hard to determine his age too. I guessed him to be between thirty-five and sixty-five. Yet, there was a feeling of familiarity I got when I looked at him; I could have sworn I'd seen or met him before.

"Alexandra," he started to say. "We do know each other—just in a different time and dimension. This is something you will eventually recognize and accept. But please, let me explain myself. We do not have much time and I need to make sure you understand the most important parts of what I have to share with you."

I already had goose bumps on my arms but remained silent for once, biting back my impulse to throw questions at him. How did he know my name?

"My name—at least, my name *here*—is Goden. It is I who summoned you and your friends." I made an expression of disbelief and he read it through and through. "Yes, Alexandra, you *are* part of the prophecy but I cannot tell you more than that. I can only guide you and assure you that I will be here when you most need me."

It was then I couldn't hold back my questions anymore and let impulse control take a vacation.

"What do you mean you can't tell me more!" I knew I sounded desperate, but I was in a desperate situation after all and didn't care. I had to know everything I could, especially if I ever wanted to see my family and home—er, planet—again. "How can you know that we're part of this so-called prophecy but can't give me more details about it?"

"Well, that is the point of a prophecy. You can be destined or called to do something, but not every detail is worked out. You see, you still have a choice regarding the decisions you make as the prophecy is fulfilled. And no, it does not become a self-fulfilling prophecy just because you know it has to do with you."

At this point, I really wondered if he had some kind of power to read my every thought. Talk about a lack of privacy. "Many different situations and outcomes can transpire through the course of your journey in being part of a new adventure. However, the outcome is certain—you *will* prevail, but how you do so is up to you and your companions. Perhaps that will bring you a little confidence." He smiled slightly and seemed to be looking beyond my eyes. Then his gaze dropped to the fire.

"So, uh, Mister...Goden. We really are on another planet and we really are part of that prophecy Chief Kodu had us listen to?"

"Yes." He looked up from the fire and became thoughtful.

"Okay. Well, let's say for argument's sake, I believe all this. Where do you fit in and can you help us? Can you get us back home?"

"I am what you would probably deem as your 'spirit guide'. You see, there is a realm of supernatural and magical happenings and on Cantelia; this realm is more open and visible than that of Earth. Many people of Earth have lost touch with their spirits and are satisfied with the visible and 'solid' objects surrounding them. Because of that, they have been blinded and deprived of all that beings with spirits are capable of.

"I am sure you must know an inkling of what I'm talking about...surely you have witnessed things beyond the natural laws of science and logical explanations? Just like you are experiencing now with your spirit being detached from your physical body. Your mind was freer when you became ill tonight and I was able to easily summon you.

"Such things like this happen all the time on this planet and because of that, evil can take control very quickly here compared to the slow and stealthy evil of the Earth. There, it deceitfully seeps itself into the hearts of mankind until everything good inside them is sucked dry. The good news is that evil here can also be overcome with a much more brutal and lasting effect—that is where you and your companions come in.

"You will of course learn more in time as you go on your journey but for the time being, I can only tell you what is absolutely crucial to your survival and success on this cursed island. Once your task here is finished, I will make sure you are sent back home. You will awake soon so I must hurry."

I listened intently as Goden explained things that were very confusing and frightening at times. He constantly reminded me to communicate all the information he gave to the rest of my group. I heartily promised, but before I could ask him for further clarification, he said, "I'm sorry I can't explain more Alexandra. Please try to remember my words to the best of your ability. I will be with you even if you can't see me. I am always watching. There are others you will meet later who will be of great service to you and your friends. I must go; dawn approaches and you will have quite a morning ahead of you.

"Two more things before I leave. First, do not trust everyone you meet. It would be very unwise if you did. Second, the more hope we can rally on this planet, the sooner we defeat the evil that is desperately trying to vanquish Cantelia."

And with that, he placed his hood back on, walked to the mouth of the cave and was gone in a flash. I called out to him but to no avail. The fire did not glow as cheerily as before and I watched it die down into nothingness—like some invisible black hole sucked it dry. The cave was completely dark and I started to panic until muffled sounds began emanating from some place far off. However, they grew louder and nearer and nearer...

Horror-movie-like screams broke through the remnants of my dream and the morning silence in our hut. I barely had time to feel groggy. "What the he—" I began to say with obvious annoyance.

I felt nowhere near well rested and my stomach was growling because it was completely empty. However, my question was cut off with screams as well. Terrified, I scrambled backwards on all fours until I hit a wall. Heather was stationed on the opposite side of the hut, trying to blend into the wall, hugging her legs to her chest.

Keira's body remained frozen in fear on her floor mat, with the exception of her mouth moving to allow the shrieks to escape. Her chin was almost touching the very top of her collar bone and her eyes were the size of ping pong balls. In the center of her chest, a very large, rainbow-colored spider crawled slowly, feeling its way around, unfazed by her deafening noises. Tears were streaming down her face and she finally articulated, "Get it off me, get it off me!"

The spider happened to be so large that I could count all ten of its legs—yes, *ten*. It was roughly the size of a squid. It looked more gruesome than anything I had had to cut out of insect catalogs for those silly science collage projects in elementary school. I guess all the colors it had were cool— kinda like being thrown in a Skittles bag or something—but I wasn't about to pick it up and make it my new pet.

Its eyes were unusually large for a spider and a haunting look danced in its pupils. Being irrationally and deathly afraid of most, if not all, bugs myself, I became paralyzed while observing the terrifying sight. This was not a bug you could just squash with a boot. This was a bug that required heavy ammo.

Though still angry with Keira from all the events of the prior night, I didn't want her to receive a potentially poisonous spider bite and become ill or face death on this cursed island. The giant arachnid raised its body high on all ten legs so that it became teepee shaped. Then I heard a wet, cracking sound and began to tremble when I witnessed the long, sharp, white...*somethings*...slowly lower from its underside. This creature had to have been some kind of sick, mutant, hybrid spider that enjoyed screaming victims to sink sharp appendages into.

I was internally arguing with my fears to get the nerve to move from my spot and help her, but thankfully, the door flung open at the very minute I decided to help. Gasping in surprise as our rescuer strode in, I couldn't decide which I would rather have had in our hut at that moment: the ginormous rainbow spider getting ready to strike Keira or the man-sized rat mumbling unintelligibly to itself while kneeling down on one knee. In particular, neither was at the top of my list—or Keira's for that matter.

"Keira," I said, my voice barely above a whisper, "Put your head down and don't move a muscle."

Spear in hand—well, paw-like-hand—the large rat bent lower, nimbly drew back his throwing arm and released the weapon with a quick flick of the wrist. The sharp point went right through the body of the spider, pinning it to the wall behind Keira's head. He had amazing aim—and just in time, too. The sharp, white somethings looked like shark teeth and were still unsheathed as a weapon.

Rainbow-colored guts were spewing out from the body as the spider wriggled for a bit and then went stiff. I looked at Keira's face and there was rainbow gunk all over her face and hair. I think she was crying. The shock of it all caused her to pass out and the sudden silence was haunting.

Heather only whimpered with eyes so wide that she looked like a bug herself. I chose to remain still and not make any sudden movements lest the giant rat decided to attack us. He popped his head back in, his nose busy with the task of sniffing deeply. He wore a short grass skirt and held a spear in his left hand—I mean, paw. Whatever.

Suddenly things were beginning to become connected for me. This rat looked exactly like the ones we had seen on the day before on the beach—human-like features included. As my brain processed all the events of the day before, including my crazy dream, I found myself more alert and awake in a short amount of time than ever before. This would be one morning where coffee would be a non-essential.

The rat man—who I now recognized as one of the tribal guards from the evening before—squeaked as low as he could and another rat person came running to our door. I could tell this one was female by its less stalky build and makeshift muumuu. She carried a small clay jar with some rough cloth threaded through the handle. Looking at both Heather and me, she slowly entered the hut and began to kneel by Keira.

"Alex! What is that thing doing?!" shrieked Heather. "Ohmigod, ohmigod..." she repeated.

"I think it, or rather, *she* is going to help clean up Keira from her buggy friend. Just chill out and watch, okay?"

Heather reluctantly nodded and we both watched as the rat woman opened up the towel and poured some water on it. Then she wrung out the excess liquid and used the cloth to start wiping off Keira's forehead. She motioned to me to come to her side, and amazingly, I found I could move.

Her hands looked warm and fuzzy and just plain weird, but she was careful not to touch mine as she handed me another towel to dip in water and help wipe the goo. I cautiously patted the damp towel around Keira's cheeks and felt for her pulse. It was rapid but steady and strong. I looked at the would-be nurse next to me.

"She'll be okay in a little bit," I said quietly. The rat woman nodded once and rose quickly. She gazed back at me before exiting our hut.

Most of the viscous material had been cleaned off Keira and I finished wiping the bits and pieces as best I could. Keira would have to wash her hair later to get the remains off. Outside, squeaky sounds shot back and forth—I could tell that the two creatures were arguing. More commotion came from farther off and Ben's voice rang loud and clear.

"Look, I don't know who—what you are, but you cannot keep us from the girls. We'll fight you if we need to; now let us through!"

All the boys—except for Geoffrey—ran at the door and practically tumbled on top of each other as they burst through the weak structure. Justin fell on top of Keira's legs, waking her up with a jolt. I couldn't help but laugh.

"Get it off me, get it off me!" she shrieked,

obviously unaware that the spider was now gone. We were all a little worse for the wear from our adventures and uncomfortable sleeping arrangements, but she won the award for total wreckage. Her hair was unkempt and wily with bits of multi-colored "gel" making her bangs go every which way, eye shadow and mascara smeared in creases around her eyes, and there were lines from the sleeping mats imprinted on her discolored cheeks—not to mention flakes of spider bits in patches all around her upper torso and head. Attractive. A few rat people peered through our doorway with looks of amusement on their furry faces. Keira accidentally kicked Justin in the ribs while he tried to pick himself up.

"Ouch!" he cried. Keira clearly lacked empathy by her failure to apologize. I suspected her shock had worn off miraculously.

"Get off me!" she yelled at a pained Justin. Sitting upright and wriggling backwards helped to free her of his body. Daniel reached down and lifted up his brother with ease and narrowed his eyes at Keira. I thought the whole episode would be over so we could talk and share about our evening in the huts, but I was sadly mistaken. Pouty Princess noticed the creatures waiting at our door and shrill screams erupted from her vocal chords. I rolled my eyes and nudged Ben.

"I liked it better when she was passed out." He chuckled at my joke and gave me a winning smile. Geoffrey grabbed a hold of the hysterical Keira and locked eyes with her.

"Shut up! Just shut up! You need to stop freaking out so we can figure out what's going on to get out of this stupid place. There's weird crap all around, so deal with it okay?"

Surprisingly, his "real talk" worked like a charm and she did indeed shut up and became subdued. Much of the tension in the small space was released and all eyes were on Geoffrey. He slowly let go of her, wiping his hands on his pants, and added, "Umm...you should probably shower or something." She simply responded with a *humph* sound.

"We *all* need to shower, but that's besides the point," said Ben. "What we need to do first is figure out how to get back home." The rat people were still hanging out in our doorway so Ben didn't say anything further. Daniel quietly strode towards them and asked if we could have some privacy.

It appeared that the rat men were not going to give in, but the female rat shook her hand-paws at them and they reluctantly backed off and shut the door. Once that was dealt with, we all let out a collective sigh and started to sit down on the mats one by one. Everyone steered clear of the forgotten spear and dead giant spider.

"Hey! They forgot the spear!" I almost shouted, but thankfully my excitement came out in a loud whisper.

Daniel's blue eyes looked around the hut and he

found one of the used towels on the ground, placing it on the dead spider with his left hand while pulling the spear out with his right. We all grimaced at the slippery and sucking sounds it made. A pungent stench like rotting onions filled the small hut. We tried best to cover our noses with our arms but it was still horrid.

Daniel handed the spear to Ben and quickly grabbed the other towel from the floor, creating a thicker cover on top of the dead insect. He wrapped it tight and we were so grateful when the smell greatly decreased. At least now it was bearable.

Meanwhile, Ben tucked the spear under Heather's sleeping mat and pushed it close to one of the walls in hopes that it would be less obvious that we were hiding a weapon. Sooner or later they'd remember and come looking for it. The door, whooshing open without warning, startled us all.

I'm sure we all looked like deer caught in headlights, but the female rat took no notice. She simply bent down and placed down a large grass woven basket with piping hot meat. Next, she put a stack of dry banana-looking leaves next to the bowl, along with a wooden container filled with some type of creamy liquid. Then, something resembling bananas was what completed the meal.

The only thing that made me question whether they were bananas or not had to be due to their color: pink. Yeah, they were *pink*. She didn't even look up this time; she kind of stooped as she turned away from us while simultaneously closing the door. We all unfroze and looked at one another.

"Well," said Heather, breaking the tension, "*that* was weird. But whatever; I'm hungry and I'm not shy so I'm just going to help myself." And with that, she grabbed a leafy plate, piled on some meat using her fingers and snapped one of the pink fruits from the rest of the bunch. Daniel and Ben were next, then Geoffrey and Justin and myself.

Keira remained in her silent tantrum until she couldn't help herself and moved to the bowl in a flash, serving herself more food than her mother would have approved of, I'm sure. She chose to sit away from our misshapen circle—perhaps because she was embarrassed of her appearance. No matter; we chose to ignore her.

"So...how did you ladies sleep?" asked Daniel. Always the charmer.

"I slept okay," answered Heather. "And Alex did too, once she stopped throwing up."

"Heather!" I complained. "I didn't exactly want to broadcast that to everyone!"

"Oh, sorry," she frowned.

"You weren't feeling good last night, Alex?" questioned Ben. I nodded my head. "That sucks. Maybe it was the food?"

"I think so," I began to say, but I stopped myself short because only Ben seemed interested. The others started talking to one another while eating. But Ben encouraged me to explain more to him.

"What happened? Do you feel better today?"

"Yeah, I do, but..."

"But what?"

"Well, have you ever had a crazy dream and you thought it could mean something—something *really* important?" I asked. He looked at me with curiosity, head slightly titled to one side.

"Umm, sure, I guess so. Why?"

"I think the dream I had last night meant something important for us; for all of us. And I think I need to share it with everyone, but I don't know if they'll listen to what I have to say. It's pretty *out* there, if you know what I mean." I desperately hoped I could share what Goden had said to me with the others, but thought it'd be wise to test it out on Ben first. I felt like I could trust him more than any of the others because he seemed more open-minded to me.

"You can tell me Alex," he replied warmly. "You can tell me anything. Besides, we're already on a different planet with giant animals that walk around on their hind legs during the day. How could your dream be any stranger than what we're seeing here?" He smiled and touched my arm. "So, tell me."

"Okay, so this is really crazy, but here goes. When I was sick last night, I kinda had this out-of-body experience, almost like a hallucination but I could control it. I could see everything happening but didn't feel sick anymore. Then I tried to get Heather and

Keira's attention but they apparently couldn't hear me. Before I knew it, I heard other sounds that were...I dunno...maybe miles off. Somehow I had this overwhelming feeling to distance myself from the sound. I didn't know where it was coming from but it seemed dangerous and I needed to get away.

"So, I walked right through that wall there and broke into a sprint where the clearing ended. I found the ocean and swam a bit to a cave where I met...*him*." I paused, not really sure where to go after that.

"Who?" Ben questioned. "Who did you meet?"

"He said his name is Goden," I continued.

"Goden?" he repeated. "That's a weird name. Sounds like one of those names that celebrities would name one of their kids."

"Anyway," I tried to hide my irritation at being interrupted. "He told me he brought us here—summoned, I think the term was. He confirmed that the prophecy Kumani read to us last night really is legit and that we supposedly are the 'Chosen Ones'. I know, I know—it sounds so ominous, but he explained quite a bit to me. Goden said that it's up to us how we go about helping out. He didn't tell me *why* it has to be us; he only told me it *is* us. For some reason, I can only remember a few things he told me—"

"Alex, I really think you should tell the others about this. And I believe you're right: there *is* something important about all this. Maybe it's exactly what we need to know in order to get back home.

Yeah?"

"Okay," I said slowly. "As long as you back me up." He nodded and gently squeezed my arm again.

"Hey, guys, listen up. Alex has something important to tell us and you need to listen. We both think it's what'll get us out of this crazy place and back on our own planet." Then he looked at me, reassuringly. "Go ahead, tell them."

I told everyone else what I had shared with Ben, then continued to finish the rest of my encounter with Goden and the whole magical/spiritual stuff. They were all intently listening and actually waited patiently until I finished.

"Oh!" I chimed excitedly towards the end of my spiel. "I almost forgot the most important thing! Okay, so you know how there're creatures outside of our hut instead of people?" They all nodded in unison.

"Well, that's the 'problem' or curse that Kodu was trying to explain to us last night. The curse is that their tribe—and the other tribes on this island for that matter—turn into animals during the day to gather food for those giant jaguars we saw on the beach yesterday. If they don't pay tribute every day, they will be hunted and killed.

"Apparently, the jaguars, who used to be a tribe here like Kodu said, are the henchmen of the head evil guy—the one responsible for the oppression of this whole planet. But they can't turn back into humans; until they have the tribes people completely surrendered to their master, they will not regain their human form. The tribes have become way smaller in population just these past few months because anyone who stands up to the giant felines has always lost.

"Unfortunately, instead of this problem uniting the tribes, they have all been blaming one another for the curse being placed upon the island instead. This makes them weaker and one of the specific instructions Goden told me was that we have to figure out how to get them all together to stand up to the bad guys so the curse can be broken. At least they haven't given up yet.

"If they can destroy their enemies and begin to hope again, that feeling of hope is supposed to be enough to release the evil guy's hold on them."

"Does that mean the other animals—the boars and cats—are under the curse too? Those are the other tribes, right?" asked Heather.

"Mmmhmm. I'm afraid so. Pretty crazy, huh?"

"So what happens if we don't accomplish all this?" Keira had surprisingly contributed to the conversation. All heads turned from her back to me.

"Umm...I guess we don't get to go home," I stated.

"Well, that's all the motivation I need! What do we need to do?" Daniel was more eager to leave this place than his twin.

"It seems we have no choice. Whether all the stuff you were told is true or not, we do need a plan of action. Maybe if we at least help the tribes work out some of their issues we can stop being prisoners and find our own way out of this place." Ben was probably right and I showed my approval by sort of slapping his leg. This made for an awkward moment...yet again. I was trying to be like one of the guys with a friendly slap, but it didn't work.

Justin asked the only obvious question left. "Where do we start?"

Ben looked in the direction of the mat that was hiding the spear and became pensive. "I think I have an idea..."

Chapter Twelve: Hunted

The hut was not reinforced with as much wood and grass as some of the others. I could see why it had been vacant and therefore the choice of our "guest" quarters. It made for a shabby shelter, especially if it rained, but this all worked to our immediate advantage. The boys examined the tiny perimeter and found a few weaker spots.

Ben's plan was to use the spear to sort of whittle down one of the bamboo crisscrosses because removing patches of dry grass would not create a wide enough space for any of us to get through.

While Ben and Daniel worked on the wall opposite the door, Heather and I tried to talk about nothing in particular—and very loudly at that too. We wanted to make sure the guards, who were probably listening, would hear only a bunch of nonsense and take their sweet time to check up on us. After a few minutes, Ben indicated that progress had been made by giving a thumbs up. Now it was time to pull away the thick, wheat-colored grass.

Geoffrey went to help and Justin joined Heather's and my conversation to hide the rustling sounds. We kept eyeing the door with nervous glances but nothing happened. Looking back to their progress, the small hole had significantly increased in size. It was low to the ground, so it should have been easy enough to crawl through.

Geoffrey tested it not even a minute later and he was through. Then Daniel crawled through and he was out. Ben grabbed Keira, put a finger to his lips to remind her to keep quiet and helped her crawl through the space. Heather, Justin and I were already in line by the time Keira's feet disappeared. Heather was next and I decided to let Justin through before me.

Once it was my turn, I noticed the freshness of the air right away. I closed my eyes for a few seconds and inhaled deeply as Daniel reached down to help me up. Everyone else was squatting to avoid being caught by wandering villagers. I turned around to help Daniel pull Ben out and then we heard them. High pitched barking sounds were the noises coming from the guards who discovered that we had just escaped.

"Run!" yelled Ben. Daniel grabbed the spear off the ground, pulled my hand in his and started to sprint.

We ran past the edge of the clearing and straight into the dense jungle. Geoffrey, who had been the forerunner of our little escapade, stopped very suddenly. "I don't know which way we should go!" he panicked. We looked behind Ben who was at the rear and could see the tips of spears bobbing up and down. I released Daniel's hand and trotted up to Geoffrey.

"I do," I said with confidence, and led them the same way I had run the night before. I followed my instincts and let my subconscious be my GPS. I thought that maybe if I got us to the cave, we'd be safe for a while. Just when I thought I couldn't run any further, the plant life became less dense and red sand particles were intermingled with the dark brown dirt of the jungle floor. There was no one behind us.

"I think we lost 'em!" exclaimed Daniel. "Let's jump in the water real quick—it'll do us all some good." I think he had meant that last statement especially for Keira but no one dared to look in her direction.

We all splashed into the water and it was absolutely divine. All the sticky, gross, dirty junk was instantly swept clean by the ocean waves and the water was the perfect temperature. For a little bit, I almost forgot I was on a whole different planet and thought of how great Spirit Lake felt in the summer time.

Just as we were getting out of the water to find a hiding place, arrows whizzed through the air out of the thick greenery and barely missed my left arm. "Look out!" screamed Geoffrey. There was nowhere to go but under the water to our certain deaths or back to the beach. Our only choice was that of surrender. It was too dangerous to try to swim to the cave. What if their arrows hit their marks?

We put our hands up and shouted, "We

surrender, we surrender!"

We trudged out of the water slowly, fingers interlaced and hands on the tops of our heads. There was no one visible. Tiny yellow glints of light sparkled through the trees and vines. When we reached the glistening red sand, our attackers swiftly popped out of their hideout, weapons drawn. The cats we had seen on the beach from yesterday were even uglier up close. The bumpy warts covering their skin in patches were hideous; I would never have wished for even my enemies to look that ugly.

With hands still on our heads, we were corralled into a very tight circle and bound with crude and scratchy rope. Even our ankles were tied close together—but not so close we couldn't walk at an average pace. Finally, after our wrists were bound, they tied us together in a line by securing rope around our waists. Then a few of the hairless creatures poked us with arrow tips and we started moving.

It was awful. We were still very wet from the ocean water and had barely had time to recover from our sprint through the jungle away from Kodu's people. At this point, I started to wish we had never escaped. Kodu at least thought we were definitely to be kept alive. Who knew what this cat tribe would do with us? I shuddered when I wondered if they were cannibals. Then I grew angry because I felt that somehow, Goden should have warned me about this. He had said he'd be around but now I started to doubt. I even began to doubt that my hallucination or dream or whatever it had been was real.

As I got lost in my thoughts, spears whizzed through the air out of nowhere. The cat leading our prison trail was just getting ready to notch an arrow and a spear hit him right through the gut. Heather screamed and Ben yelled, "Get down you guys!"

We immediately obeyed. A few more cats were killed until those remaining threw down their bows and arrows and put their partly human hands up. Four warrior rats became visible as they swung down from the trees, Tarzan style—but without the loud yell. Three of them grabbed a hold of the surrendered felines and added them to our prison chain with their own ropes. The other one came to look at us and shook his head in what I assumed to be disbelief. There was something strangely familiar about his features.

"Kumani?" I asked. He nodded. I held out my poor wrists and questioned, "Will you cut us loose?" I tried a smile, hoping he'd cut the uncomfortable contraptions right away. Instead, he only shook his head a definite *no* and chattered to the other rats accompanying him. Two took the rear and one came up to the front with him. It looked like we would be going back to the very place we had fled only moments ago. This really sucked.

Onward we trekked and in less than thirty minutes, we were back at square one. At least they shoved us back into one hut together—the boys' hut instead of ours with a gaping hole in the back. The tribesmen took no chances though and doubled our guard detail by placing a rat on each side of the dwelling. It was good to know that we were still of some use to them, being the "Chosen Ones" and all. However, I'm sure we all feared Kodu's reaction to our antics when he received word upon his arrival back to the village.

Just as we were settling down on woven mats and rubbing our sore wrists, the door opened and piping hot food was delivered. It was more meat—no surprise there—with some leafy greens and very bright, purple fruit. The boys wasted no time in grabbing at all the grub with greedy eyes. "Hey, save some for us!" piped in Heather.

While we ate, Daniel began the conversation. "So...how are we gonna get out of here for real?" He looked around at each of us but only I looked back. I think everyone else was skeptical and discouraged by the day's events.

"To be blunt, I don't think we're gonna get out of here until we do what they want—or until we do what Goden advised. I know it sounds crazy, but maybe there really is a reason why we're here. If there is, it's probably the least crazy part about this whole escapade so far."

That actually grabbed some attention from my companions and Geoffrey gave me the most annoying look of disbelief. I could have kicked myself for still thinking he was attractive at the same time.

"Well Geoffrey, I think that whatever course we choose, it has something to do with reuniting the tribes so they can kick this curse themselves. I got the feeling that we're not supposed to solve all their problems for them but be like...well, like guides or something. Maybe we need to help them get over their differences and that will be a start." I had never felt so unsure in my life and Geoffrey certainly fueled my insecurities.

"You have a feeling? A *feeling*? How can we go off that? I'd like to get home before, oh, I don't know—before I die of old age! This is total bull. You expect us to go off a hunch from some supposed special dream or food poisoning hallucination to get us out of here? You are insane if you think that's a plan I'm on board for!"

I felt about three inches tall and began to sink low, fighting back tears of anger and rejection. To my surprise, Ben stood up for me.

"Look Geoff, maybe it's a crazy idea to follow a hunch but do *you* have another idea that'll get us out of here? Yeah, didn't think so. So shut up and sit down." Geoffrey was starting to stand up, but Ben's words made him sit right back down.

"You may intimidate people at school, but here, you're just as unimportant and lost as the rest of us. If we want to ever see our families and homes again, the only thing we have is this encounter Alex had. Unless one of us has a rocket ship in our pockets, I suggest we give her our full and cooperation and contribute help in any way we can. That includes you too, Keira." Keira's eyes almost bulged out of their sockets, but she had nothing to retort. Maybe miracles were starting to happen.

Though you could feel this awful, growing tension in the small room, I swallowed my tears and my pride and we all huddled in to figure out a plan. Perhaps an hour later, we had hashed out some okay, mediocre, and just plain stupid ideas. The gist was to get all three of the tribes to somehow meet without killing one another, help them to see that they all had a common goal and that only by them working together could they get rid of the curse. Easy, right?

"I, for one, don't see how any of this will happen unless we have the chief on our side, or at least his permission to gather everyone together. Besides, he's the one who knows their locations and customs and he views us as the 'Chosen Ones'. For all we know, the other tribes could be cannibals and would only see us as their next dinner party, minus the party." Heather shuddered at her own words.

"And who knows if they speak any English?" Justin made a good point.

"Okay...so what you're saying is we need to find a diplomatic way to approach Kodu and see if we can convince him to go along with our idea?" Daniel's tone was clearly rhetorical.

"I'm just worried about Keira's boyfriend telling him about our little adventure this morning and his reaction too..."

"He is *not* my boyfriend!" Keira was very heated and directed every particle of anger at Ben.

"If you want me to go along with this, don't insult me and make up crap."

She moved to one of the corners with her arms crossed, a frown firmly set on her sleep-deprived face. I could picture a tiara popping out of nowhere and resting on her head.

"You're right, you're right—my bad, Keira. I shouldn't have said that. I think we're all a little worn out and frustrated and I didn't need to take a blow at you. Let me rephrase: I am worried that Kumani is gonna tattle on us—or one of the guards will for sure—and that'll down our chances of Kodu putting faith in us." Ben ruffled his hair for the millionth time. I think it was a habit he did when he was in deep thought or nervous or both.

"Yeah, but we have to try. We just *have* to. What else can we do?" I tried not to sound too desperate but I don't think it worked.

"We could just walk out." And with that, Geoffrey was an idiot and pulled hard on the door of the hut. It flew open with a wooden *clank* while he strode about two feet before getting smacked in the face with a furry paw-hand and was hit on the top of the head with the blunt end of a spear. We all stayed seated in our circle, watching the whole scene transpire. In reality, it happened very quickly but I, for one, saw it in slow motion and actually felt bad for the guy. No one got up to help him. He was out cold.

The rat guards dragged him back in to the hut by the collar and underarms and weren't very gentle when settling him on a woven mat. They squeaked something to another guard immediately outside the door and he came back in minutes with a female rat. I recognized her as the same one from the morning. She must have thought I was the Florence Nightingale of the group because she motioned for me to come and help her.

There was a wooden pitcher of water and some rough cloth which I assumed were for helping to stop the gruesome bleeding of Geoffrey's broken nose. The girls looked away and I slowly untangled my legs, awkwardly crawling to her. I muttered curses under my breath and stopped feeling sorry for him. How far would my sense of compassion be tested on this trip?

She guided my hands with her rough and fuzzy ones; it was like a having a very hairy cactus hold mine. I tried not to make a face from the uncomfortable feeling it gave me while allowing her to move the cloth we held together in small, wiping motions. She finally let go and watched for a while as I got the rest of the blood off Geoffrey's face. Deep red, congealed goo sat in his nostrils but at least fresh blood had stopped pouring out. Perhaps it was due to the swelling, now very evident around his nose and eyes.

"I think his nose is broken," I said more to

myself than to anyone else. The rat woman looked at me curiously and then placed a damp, fresh cloth on Geoffrey's forehead and left it there. She patted my arm in a reassuring way, gathered the soiled materials and water pitcher and exited the hut. The light had changed inside; less of the suns' rays came through the high windows. I could almost feel sunset approaching.

Perhaps that was part of the curse: that those on the island would feel when sunset would take place because it meant that they would be back in their own bodies for the night. I left Geoffrey's side to join the others.

"He's still breathing, so I guess he'll be okay." Everyone looked at me like I had said we weren't going to have a turkey for Thanksgiving. "What?!"

"You didn't have to help him like that, you know," Daniel said.

"Oh," I replied. "I know. I just didn't think anyone else would, so I stepped up." There was a faint smile tugging at my lips.

"Alex, I'm sorry we've been so stubborn. We will all try harder to listen to what you have to say. I mean, I know you're trying your best—better than any of us— to get us home. We're all behind you. Right guys?" Daniel looked specifically at Keira.

"Yeah," everyone muttered in unison.

"Well, thanks guys. That means a lot...really, it does," I replied. We sat in the quiet, darkened hut for a bit before my mind switched gears. "The sun has set.

All the tribesmen will be back soon," I whispered. As if I cued him, Kumani opened the door at that moment, clearly back in his beautiful, yet arrogant human form. This greatly brightened Keira's face but made the rest of us anxious. He did not look very pleased to see us either.

"What were you thinking—trying to run away?" he asked in a seething tone. "Did you think you could escape? You do not know the jungle and the dangers it holds. You could have been killed by the men of Feldor!" Boy, was he *mad*. But surprisingly, he seemed to show more concern for our well being than anything else.

"You're so right, Kumani," Keira's voice dripped with heavy flirtation. "We were so stupid, so foolish, so..."

"Can it, Keira." Ben's patience had clearly run out. "Look, Kumani, you're right, we were stupid. And desperate too. We just want to get home but it's clear that Kodu wants our help before that happens. I guess you're gonna tell him what happened—or does he already know?"

"No," Kumani replied with a little less heat. "He does not need to know. He has enough to worry about. I have instructed the guards to remain silent about your actions from today. But this is the only time, do you understand?"

"Clear as day," Daniel said, a little too sarcastically.

Tamar Hela

"There is another problem. The men we captured today—the cats who took you—may be killed tonight by the chief's orders. One man is Akeen, the son of Feldor and the one to marry my cousin, Resina. Kodu believes Akeen kidnapped Resina and if he cannot find out about her from Akeen tonight, Kodu will burn him to death. Before the chief questions Akeen, he would like you to come to the meeting hut. He thinks maybe you can tell if Akeen is telling the truth or not. His life may be in *your* hands tonight."

"Great," whined Heather. "I don't even have a driver's permit yet and I'm supposed to decide if someone gets to live or not? What kind of sick place are you running here?"

"I do not understand what you mean, Heather," started Kumani, "But if you think that this is a serious matter, you are correct. While you wait to be called by my uncle, I will take you young women to another hut where some of the women are waiting to help you bathe and change for tonight."

I looked warily at the boys while rising from the grass mat. They only shrugged in sync, except for Geoffrey. He was still passed out on the ground. Heather, Keira and myself followed after Kumani— some of us in greater haste than others. He paused at the doorframe and looked back at the semi-disfigured face of Geoffrey, shaking his head back and forth.

"Fool," he muttered quietly and turned to lead us outside. For once, I shared his exact sentiment.

Feast Island

On our way to the bathing hut, Kumani asked us about the spear we used to escape in the morning and we shared with Kumani the horrors of the giant spider. We learned that it actually had a name: Kongulo. Thinking about it once again made me shudder. He took notice.

"Yes, they can be dangerous, but we are used to them here. The best thing to do is to stay quiet." I lifted an eyebrow at Keira, but she was gushing at Kumani and had no clue I was staring at her.

Bathing, rather *"bathing"* was interesting. Since we weren't trusted to go out to any nearby bodies of water, we had to sponge bath it. I didn't have enough time to truly feel violated; each one of us was quickly washed down by half a dozen tribeswomen and they were very nonchalant about the whole ordeal. Thankfully, they had others washing our clothes and hanging them out to dry. I was beginning to feel almost human again.

Heather, Keira and I were treated like dolls—primped and fussed over—when it came to getting ready for another large feast planned for the evening. Adorned in modest but traditional tribal garb gave me some hope that perhaps the chief really had no clue about our near escape just hours before and that maybe, just maybe, we were still in good standing and could find a way back home soon. But then I remembered the decision we would be a part of later and my stomach tightened. I didn't want someone's blood on my hands. I mean, I hadn't even gone to a high school dance yet.

Dinner consisted of more piles of steaming, delicious meat placed on large leaves. According to the boys, Geoffrey was still recovering in their hut, unable to attend both dinner and the meeting to come. He also missed out on bath-time. The boys were now almost as clean as we girls were.

A sort of fruit medley was served as our dessert and the drinks must have been somewhat fermented because I was feeling slightly woozy and *really good* about everything. In fact, my current state was so relaxed that it didn't cross my mind to freak out when Kumani came for us to go before Kodu. To my relief, the chief appeared pretty happy to see us. We met in the same large hut from the first meeting.

On the floor was a gagged and limb-tied body; I assumed it to be Akeen, the son of the chief of the cat tribe. His eyes were sad and I came to the conclusion that he had no fight left in him at this point. Though he had captured us earlier that day, I couldn't help be feel sorry for the guy.

Something inside me was suggesting to do all that was in my power to save him from death at the hands of Kodu. It was apparent that Kodu had ordered him to be tortured already. Perhaps this was what Goden alluded to in our meeting the prior night. My instincts rarely led me astray and I trusted my gut feeling on this one.

Feast Island

Ata, the old sage, was present at our meeting, along with some older tribe members. The large crowd from the night before was significantly reduced to less than a dozen men. Someone new was present, however. I recognized him as Kodu's brother, Falu. He flanked Kodu's right. Strange that he hadn't shown up the night before. His demeanor said very clearly that he was not very happy to be attending.

The six of us were still hovering near the doorway behind Kumani. The chief looked to our group, beckoning us closer with hand motions. Daniel took the natural position of leader and we followed, practically at his heels. We all waited for the chief or Kumani to speak first. I noticed that Kumani was looking at Akeen with utter contempt and hatred. This seemed somewhat out of character for him and that worried me.

"Come closer, young ones," Kodu began. "That Akeen." He nodded in disgust toward the pathetic and miserable young man on the floor.

"He say he don't take Resina. I think he lie. You help me and tell if he lie or I kill him." Though he spoke with broken English and it sounded a little funny, the matter itself was not laughable.

His meaning had such finality and I knew killing Akeen would somehow make things worse. I had to stop this...but how? Without thinking, I tugged on Daniel's arm and pulled him down a bit to whisper in his ear. He understood and nodded quickly, keeping his gaze on the chief the whole time.

"Chief Kodu, may I have permission to speak?"

"Yes."

"Since last night, there have been some...uh...new developments. Alex here has had a sort of vision and she would like permission to tell you about it." I watched the chief's expression the whole time, trying to figure out if he was willing to listen to me or otherwise.

What I didn't expect was for Ata to get up, point his walking stick at me and say, "You speak." Apparently, I had a willing audience after all.

Still feeling some of the warm fuzzies from the drinks at dinner, I straightened up and didn't have to think twice about what I was going to say. It all flowed—like it wasn't me or like someone was speaking through me. "Chief Kodu, Ata, other tribesmen...I had a dream last night and I met Goden."

Once I said his name, they all spoke in quick, hushed whispers, faces in shock at what I had said. But Ata banged the stick hard on the raised wooden platform and the room quieted again. I could almost hear everyone breathing—it was that quiet. Ata looked at me and nodded once in encouragement for me to continue.

"I think that my...uh...*spirit* met with his. He told me who he was and confirmed some of the things happening on this island—that the seven of us are supposed to help you become free of the curse placed upon your people *and* the other tribes. He was very clear when he spoke about the three tribes of this island to work together and I think it would be a bad idea to kill Akeen. I think Akeen is speaking the truth—he really doesn't know where Resina is. But, I think if your tribe can work together with the other two and stand up to the evil people trying to turn you against each other, you will find your daughter and can have peace again." I wasn't even sure why I had said that last part, but it sounded right.

"I disagree," interjected Kumani, before anyone could even react to my speech. "I think Akeen is telling lies and that we should kill him. The other tribes have done nothing but destroy our people and now, because of them, my beautiful cousin is gone. If we kill Akeen, it will show our strength to them. They hate us and will never change. They should all be killed before they kill us."

He then continued speaking in their native tongue in a heated and fast-paced manner. This didn't fare well with my instincts and I knew I needed to be bold and intercede or we would be going down the wrong path—and possibly risk never getting back home again. Some of the men in the room looked like they preferred siding with Kumani on the issue. Was it too late?

"Chief, no offense to Kumani, but I think he is mistaken," I blurted out. "It is *really* important that no more bloodshed happen at the hands of any tribe—

whether man or woman. Goden said the curse would only be lifted if everyone was united in a stand against the evil things prowling this island. I know that the other tribes are just as suspicious of you and hateful, but don't you think it would be a good idea to have peace again? There is strength in numbers and in order to defeat those taking your people, your food— your way of life—you are going to need all the help you can get. Surely you can see this because you have experienced war and peace and have learned much from both? I know you will make the right decision but I urge you to listen to what Goden has told me." And then I added, "Please."

Kumani gave me a dark, threatening look, but I don't think anyone else caught it. I glared back. He was becoming less and less popular in my book. Were I not as mature, I probably would have stuck my tongue out at him too.

"What you say, brother?" Kodu looked to his right and Falu squinted his eyes tight.

"Kill him," he stated darkly.

Chapter Thirteen: Visions

My heart raced quickly when I heard his words. Did the chief respect his brother so much as to kill someone due to a response like that? Instead of responding to Falu, Kodu stood and leaned close to Ata, clearly discussing the arguments Kumani, Falu, and I had delivered. In my mind, I was trying to will Kodu to side with me. I also said a silent prayer to Goden because it seemed appropriate.

A shroud of tension blanketed the room, discouraging audible discussion. Kumani looked ready to beat Akeen to death if the word was spoken. He kept cracking his knuckles and balling his hands into fists— a very different picture from the Kumani we had met the night before.

Finally, the chief faced us, a look of slight disappointment on his face. "Ata say I should trust you. We don't kill Akeen—for now." His tone was aggressive but I tried not to let that bother me.

Immediately, the guards at the back of the room strode up to Akeen and dragged him out. I let out a huge sigh of relief, noticing that my whole body had become tense while we waited to hear his fate.

"Thank you, chief," I simply said. I didn't want to press my luck by speaking any further. As I finished stating my gratitude, I dared to look in Falu's direction. He clearly was not pleased with the idea of keeping Akeen alive but remained quiet.

"Chosen Ones," Kodu started to say slowly. "I know not how we work with other tribes. I fear they take more of my people or kill us all. We talk again tomorrow. I wish to talk to Ata tonight. You go back to huts." Since there was obviously no room for argument, we turned around to walk out the door, Kumani leading yet again. He was definitely brooding, walking at a fast and furious pace. I chose to stay at the end of our little procession. The warriors behind me seemed safer than the one up front.

We said good night to the boys and I encouraged them to make sure Geoffrey was still alive. Then we were escorted to the neighboring hut and used the crude basins filled with water to wash before going to sleep. The glow of torches outside our windows barely illuminated our living space, so we were each given a sort of candle that provided just enough light to perform pre-sleep duties. Keira was using some type of boned utensil to comb through her hair and Heather and I were sitting on our mats, chatting about the day's events. A few minutes later, we heard a knock on the door. "Come in," responded Heather.

It was Kumani, holding some kind of tray with

cups on it, a smile now gracing his face. His whole demeanor had changed in a matter of minutes. That worried me. But nonetheless, he walked in slowly, closing the door behind him and kneeled down to be eye level with us. "I am sorry for how I acted tonight," he said, looking directly at me. "I was angry because I fear for my cousin. But I believe you are right—we need to work together to bring peace once again to the island. Can you forgive me?"

Though I remained skeptical, I softly uttered an "Uh...yeah," and mustered a small smile. He beamed back at me and looked at the other girls.

"Good. I brought you all something to help you sleep well tonight. Don't worry—it is a special plant that helps you sleep deeply without any bad effects." I think he had noticed Heather and I raising our eyebrows. "I drink it myself when I have had a hard day. It has a nice taste—you will like it; just try it." Well, how could we argue with that? Keira, of course, was the first to scramble right up to him and took one of the crude, wooden cups and daintily took a sip.

"Mmm...that *is* good! Thank you so much, Kumani." My stomach churned in disgust at her overly sweet tone. Ick. He simply smiled back at her. Heather and I took a chance and grabbed the remaining cups, drinking a little more heartily than Keira. It actually tasted great—not too sweet but not very watery either. It reminded me of limeade with mint and honey added to it. Yum.

"Thanks a lot Kumani," Heather began. "It is pretty refreshing and it's no secret we all need better sleep tonight."

"You are welcome. Drink all of it or it will not work as well. Now please, get some rest and stay out of trouble tomorrow. I cannot promise I will be able to save you again if you are captured by the other, more bloodthirsty tribes." Then he looked at Keira. "Perhaps I can show you some flowers tomorrow evening, when we return from our gathering?"

"I would love that!" she practically squealed.

"Very good. Now, I wish you all a good sleep." With that, he quickly got up, collected our cups, and left us alone. I laid down on my mat, yawning and stretching. Saying our day had been long and stressful was an understatement. Weariness attacked me without warning and I could barely respond back to Heather's "Goodnight." Kumani hadn't been kidding when he said the foreign concoction was a sleeping aid.

That night, my body slept deeply, but my mind was active. I had strange dreams that were very hallucinatory. Goden was calling my name at times and trying to give me messages, but it seemed that my mind was clouded. It felt like he was trying to warn me or tell me something important but I could never decipher exactly what it was. At one point, I could have sworn that someone came into our hut in the middle of the night but dismissed the thought. Finally, the endless stream of images ceased and I did get to rest completely. Before I knew it, sunshine was peeking into our small abode and Heather was gently shaking me.

"Just five more minutes," I said groggily.

"Alex, wake up. Keira's gone."

While the teenagers rested their tired minds, Kodu recalled the upsetting and painful conversation that few witnessed. Moments after the meeting hut cleared, the chief, his brother, and Ata remained. While the wise sage reassured Kodu that he had made the right decision, Falu interrupted with an impatient outburst.

"Why do you listen to that old fool?!" he said accusingly. "Send him out!" Though Kodu trusted Ata more than his brother, he obliged but shot Falu a weary look.

"Ata, please, leave us for now. I will speak with you tomorrow."

"I will leave. But know this," here, he looked directly at and pointed a crooked finger to the chief's brother. "When the poison of false glory completely consumes your heart, you will not survive. There will be no one here on this island who can or who will save you. You have turned hope against you."

"Leave us, old man!" Falu was now completely outraged, his face the brightest shade of red before it turns violet. Ata slowly made his way off the platform, leaving quietly. Once his small frame disappeared from the doorframe, Kodu broke the terse silence.

"Brother, I know you do not always trust what Ata says, but for you to disrespect him...that is unacceptable. Though you are my own flesh and blood, I will never stand for lack of control such as that in my tribe."

"I am sorry, brother," Falu replied, though his biting tone implied that he lacked any true penitent feelings. "I am sick and tired of his accusations and lack of judgment. If he really is as wise as you think, he should have advised you to kill the son of Feldor when you had the chance. You know he would kill any one of our people without thinking about it. Now we will appear weak to them and weak to our own people. Let the boy's death serve as a reminder of our strength," he urged.

"Falu," Kodu sounded tired. "You really believe that killing him will bring back my daughter? Do you think it will keep the other tribes from attacking us when they can? Will it end this curse?!" Now his voice was rising in decibels as he loosened his tight reign on his emotions. Thinking of his missing daughter always contributed to the loss of his self-control. However, he regained his composure and lowered his voice.

"I do not pretend that it would be my natural choice to kill the boy. However, I trust Ata; he has never led me astray and I will do what he says—for now. You must trust me."

"I used to trust you..." Falu trailed off, temporarily lost in thought.

"But now, I don't know you any more. What happened to the ruthless warrior I once knew? The one I looked up to? He is no longer who I see in front of me and I do not want a part of him any more."

"Surely you do not mean that brother?"

"I do. It is time for me to go elsewhere. I can no longer support your lack of judgment and see you give all your power to that old fool."

Falu turned away quickly and rushed out of the hut. Kodu could only stand there dumbfounded. He and his brother had experienced disagreements before, but this was...different. Very different than the Falu he knew. It made the chief's heart heavy and he sat back down again to ponder the unexpected exchange before going to bed.

When Ata left the hut, he took a walk through the jungle by himself. He needed time to think. Perhaps stargazing would help. After twenty minutes, he found the familiar clearing and sat cross-legged.

All the signs were present. Something had changed in the constellations and the stars were practically dancing with their message. Closing his eyes, he employed the usual technique of clearing his mind, making it ready for meditation.

Sometimes he was successful in complete separation of mind and spirit, but sometimes nothing happened. He felt that tonight would be different, however. Surely the spirits would be on his side, ready to guide him in the right direction. There were pressing matters on hand and time was running out.

An ancient chant came to his mind; it was one his grandfather taught him as a child. Using intuition only, he began to repeat the words over and over until he felt a gush of wind surround him. Opening his eyes, he recognized immediately that his spirit had separated from his body. Then a voice gave him a command.

"Ata, come," it simply said.

He knew exactly where to go and ran quickly through the foliage until he reached the water. Across the small inlet, he could see the cave and it was glowing brightly.

Having an out-of-body experience was nothing new to Ata. He only had to concentrate and ran across the water, reaching the mouth of the cave in seconds. *Finally*, he thought. *The Great Spirit has called me.*

When he entered, he was only surprised to see that the wise men of the other tribes were present in spirit too. The third presence was clearly the Great Spirit; he was glowing brightly. "Welcome, Ata," the Sprit said. "We have waited for you."

"Thank you, Great Spirit. What is it you would

have me do?" replied Ata.

"You, Nazoo, and Lanar must help your tribes unite to fight Vang and his men. If you cannot get your people to cooperate, you will all die at the hands of his tribe. There will be a battle tomorrow night; that is the only chance you have to save yourselves and the island as you know it."

"Great Spirit," questioned Nazoo, "how can we convince our people to work together? You know how stubborn they are! What are we to do?"

"You must lead by example and truly exercise your authority as their wise men. If you can each lead your tribes to the beach tomorrow night, and even convince a few of them to follow, you can save yourselves. The Chosen Ones will help you and the Brotherhood will come to fight alongside you. It will not be an easy task, but there is always hope. Take heart and follow the signs."

Ata asked one more question. "The girl, Resina—is she alive?"

"See for yourself," the Spirit replied. He stepped aside to reveal a young woman lying on the ground, bound at the ankles and wrists. She was asleep, lines of worry and stress etched into her beautiful features. "It is not too late. She can be saved, but you all must act quickly if you want to spare more lives."

The Spirit suddenly became transparent and vanished completely. Ata felt another rush of wind and his spirit was pulled from the cave in fast motion, nearly slamming back into his body. He came to with a startled jolt and opened his eyes.

The jungle was peaceful and quiet as if nothing extraordinary was taking place. Only the rustle of leaves and rhythmic noises of nocturnal insects could be heard. Ata used his walking stick to rise from his seated position and slowly made his way back to the village.

Chapter Fourteen: Missing

Someone was still trying to talk to me and I wanted to punch her in the face. "Keira's missing," Heather repeated. With all the strength I could muster, I opened my heavy eyelids just a sliver. My brain was still in the fog of morning grogginess and I could barely process Heather's words.

"Huh?" I responded grumpily. "Maybe she went to the bathroom or something. Let me sleep a bit longer, 'kay?" I flipped over to my other side and closed my eyes again. But Heather was persistent. I was *so not* a morning person.

"Alex, you don't understand—I think she's missing. Her mat is cold, like she's been gone for hours *and* I've been semi-awake for quite a while and she wasn't here. She sleeps in longer than you. I know she's not the most fun person to be around, but at the least, we should probably check with the guards and see if they know where she is."

Yawning, I let out a garbled "fine" and flopped my hand in the direction of the door. Morning sign language was all I could produce. Heather stood up and slowly approached the door. She opened it a crack and I could hear her questioning the guards. They both peered in, as if to verify her story, and became wide-eyed when they looked at Keira's empty mat. Chattering quickly, in squeaky tones, they both entered the hut and did a full scan of the small space. They examined corners and windows. As they combed the small hut, I began to take the situation a little more seriously. Then last night's conversation between Keira and Kumani flitted through my memory bank.

"Hey," I said rather abruptly, causing everyone to jump. "Didn't Kumani say he wanted to take Keira out to the jungle or something?"

"I remember he said that he would take her tonight," answered Heather.

"Hmm...you're right. But maybe he decided to take her early. She's wanted some one-on-one time with Kumani since she's laid eyes on him, so you know she wouldn't have let us know when she was leaving. Besides, she doesn't strike me as someone who follows the rules of common courtesy."

"Maybe..." Heather began. "I dunno...I guess that's the best explanation we have. We'll have to wait until later this afternoon or evening to see if they come back. I can't shake this worried feeling I have. And do you really think she'd go with him while he's transformed into a rat?"

"I think she'll take whatever form of Kumani she can get. Look, Heather, Keira's a big girl; she can figure it out," I said. I was so tired of wasting my time on her and Geoffrey.

After the guards left, Heather and I spent most of the morning in our hut, breakfast delivered just like the day before. We talked about the cute boys at school, how lame it was that everything in town was at least twenty minutes away, and about her adjusting to Pollock Pines because she had been born and raised in Los Angeles. I could definitely empathize; I missed the Bay Area all the time. Lost in thought, I jolted when the door opened. It was only someone coming in to clear our bowls and bring more water. Heather sighed.

"I suppose they're not taking any chances during the day and plan on keeping the boys in their own hut." It was more of a statement but I chose to agree with her by responding aloud.

"Yeah, you must be right. Even though he's an idiot, I wonder how Geoffrey is doing..."

"Do you like him, Alex?"

"No," I responded quickly—perhaps a little *too* quickly. I tried to look very nonchalant but Heather was no dummy.

"Oh come on, I see how you stare at him *and* you're the one who ran to his rescue the quickest yesterday. It's okay; I won't tell anyone," she only looked half serious. I started to fabricate some complicated lie but considered that perhaps she would leave me alone if I simply told the truth.

"Okay, okay. I don't *like* him. And don't get me

wrong—I think he's super hot and all, but...he really is not my type. I mean, call me picky, but I'm not into the narcissistic jerky types. Ya know?"

"Hmm...okay, fair enough. Everyone and their uncle's mother's niece have a crush on that hottie. It's really too bad he doesn't have a nice personality to go with his looks. Such a waste of beauty."

"Yeah, tragic," I agreed half-heartedly.

Lunch came and went and soon, the outside light was beginning to fade. In a matter of minutes, the tribesmen would return, back in their human forms, and we'd find out where Keira had disappeared to all day.

When darkness blanketed the village, I found it relieving to see human heads popping into our doorway motioning us out to dinner. We went to our newly usual spot and had a different type of meat waiting for us. The boys were already eating and Ben smiled when he saw us.

"Hey guys! It was so boring today without an adventure," he joked. "How you guys doing? You alright?"

"Yeah, we're fine," I responded. "We were pretty bored today too, but there's only so much dirt floor tic-tac-toe one can play." I returned his smile and immediately felt better.

He had such a reassuring manner about him; it put everyone around him at ease and feeling at ease was exactly what I needed at the moment. But when I noticed Geoffrey, all those calm feelings escaped immediately and every muscle in my body tensed. He had a brooding look that said *stay* away. Nevertheless, I chose to be kind and reach out. Brownie points for me.

"Hi Geoffrey; how ya doing?" I didn't anticipate an answer—honestly—but he surprised me by supplying one.

"I...I heard you helped me a lot yesterday. Well, uh...um, I...thanks. My nose would have been even worse if it wasn't for you."

"Wow, uh...you're welcome. I was just doing what anyone else would do in that situation. I wasn't going to let you suffer."

"Well, still. I know I can be a jerk and I appreciate that you did what you did." He smiled for a few seconds then looked away.

I left it at that, allowing his unexpected gratitude to sink in. His nose did look significantly better. You could tell that it was healing from a break but it would have been worse without the care he received. He had two semi-black eyes but still had one of the prettiest faces I'd ever seen. Heather leaned over and whispered something while I thought about the other day.

"You're staring again, Alex." I felt my cheeks growing warm and looked away quickly, hoping he wouldn't notice. Dan startled me with a question, but I welcomed anything to help me escape from a semi-awkward moment.

"Hey, where's Keira? She coming?"

"Uh, actually, she's been gone all day long," answered Heather. "Alex thinks she ran off with Kumani for the day, but I think she's missing." Her tone was chastising but I refused to feel guilty.

"I just think it's in her character to do something rude like run off for the day and fail to tell anyone. That's all."

"You know," began Ben, "Alex is probably right, Heather. That girl thrives off attention and I'm sure she's probably headed back with Kumani by now." I gave Heather an I-told-you-so look and started eating my dinner. I thought for sure that Ben and I were right and that we'd see Keira approaching any minute, hanging on Kumani's arm.

But Keira didn't show up after dinner. For the first time that day, I actually began to worry. Though she was irresponsible and severely self-absorbed, she knew better than to stay out this long. I looked around to see if Kumani had come back with the others, but couldn't spot him.

"Guys...I think Keira would have been back by now. Do you think we should ask Chief Kodu about it? I don't see Kumani anywhere either."

"It wouldn't hurt," replied Daniel. "He's sitting over there with the old guy. What's his name again?"

"Ata," Heather corrected. "C'mon, guys, let's go talk to them."

Kodu looked please to see us as we approached. "Chosen Ones, welcome. Sit." He indicated the empty grass mats near him. We sat close to him, in a jumble, and Daniel spoke first—as usual.

"Chief, may I have permission to speak?" Always so eloquent, that Daniel.

"Yes, speak young one," he said.

"We're worried about Keira. See, she hasn't been here all day long and now that it's getting late, well...we wondered if you happen to know where she is?" The chief frowned.

"I not know. Kumani and Falu not here. Falu mad I don't kill Akeen and now he gone. I think Kumani go with him...I think they go to Evil Ones."

We were all shocked to hear Kodu's theory and I feared the worst for Keira. Heather shared with the chief and Ata how strange it was that Kumani had come into our hut the night before and gave us something to drink to "help us sleep." When Ata heard this, he spoke to Kodu.

"Ata say that not good. He say Kumani maybe take girl in night."

"Why does he think that?" questioned Ben.

"Because...Falu and I fight last night. He angry with me for doing what Ata say. Ata think he want to fight against all tribes." The chief was clearly burdened. I had to intervene if we were ever going to see Keira again. Every minute that went by would be a waste. An idea struck me and I couldn't remember if it was just a notion or something that Goden told me when we met.

"Look, I know this might be hard for you to hear, but do you think that your brother could be the one behind the kidnapping of your daughter? Do you think that if we find them and Keira, we'll find Resina?"

It was a bold move to speak like this to Kodu, but he *did* think we were "chosen" for some higher purpose so perhaps he would listen. Ata leaned close to him and spoke in his ear before we heard the chief's response.

"Ata say you are right. We must find them to find answers. He have dream from the Spirits. We go tonight. I give you weapons but you stay with us. Do not run or my men shoot you." *Okay, that's incentive enough to obey orders...*

"It seems we have no choice then but to go with you. Except, you must know that we'll take Heather and Alex too. The girls go with us or we stay here," Daniel stated. The chief squeezed his eyes shut for a moment but said nothing.

"Okay," said Ata. "Come now."

The whole village was in a frenzy within minutes. The older women stayed behind with the young children, but all the other women grabbed spears and joined the rather good-sized crowd of male warriors.

We were close to Kodu, near the front. He

allowed some of the more stalky warriors to precede us. When we walked away from the village and into deeper forest, I noticed that the tiny plants on the jungle floor were glowing. I wished I could have stopped to take it all in and really enjoy all the amazing things surrounding us, but we had serious business to attend to.

Only the hum of hidden insects could be heard over the monotonous melody of quiet marching. Who knew if we were even headed in the right direction? However, I had to trust that the warriors knew what they were doing. But it might have been too late by the time things were discovered.

I stopped myself from thinking negatively and chose instead to put all my efforts into walking, wondering if I would have the guts to spear someone— or something—injuring them at the least. Not paying attention, I accidentally ran into Geoffrey.

"Sorry," I mumbled quickly. But he only grabbed me by the shoulders and put a finger to his lips so I would get the hint to shut up.

The front of our party crouched low, right before a clearing of beach and ocean. Someone made a low whistling sound and everyone surrounding us squatted low to the ground. Geoffrey followed suit and pulled me down with him abruptly. I nearly fell on my face but he held me steady and firm.

Once acclimated to a mostly uncomfortable position, I looked across those in front of me toward the clearing. At first, I found it nearly impossible to see anything. But then I thought I saw a flash of something bright and yellow. Could it just have been something like fireflies? *No, they're too steady to be bugs.*

Then it hit me: *The cat tribe! But wouldn't they be in their human form? Perhaps they retain the same type of eyes even when they're not cats...*Surely that made sense. Some of Kodu's people had dark eyes just like their rat forms. Maybe this curse had left some permanent "damage" on its victims. Suddenly, an arrow whizzed through the air and landed on a tree trunk about three feet higher than where most of heads floated.

"I don't think they missed on purpose. They're trying to warn us," Geoffrey whispered. No one moved. We waited for an eternity—well, okay, about thirty seconds, but *still.* Some in the front stayed in their crouched position and sort of crab walked a little further. Bad idea. A shower of arrows rained upon us, hitting the tree trunks lower and lower each time.

Geoffrey pushed me flat on the ground and kept his arm around me. I held fast to my spear and half choked on dirt. Boy, were we in for it now. Then someone shouted in his native tongue and there was an instant ceasefire. Only Kodu stepped forward boldly, without his spear, and hands held high in the air. I couldn't even guess what was next, but it would definitely make for an interesting turn of events.

Feast Island

Chapter Fifteen: Unexpected Help

"Graffias, bring in that pitiful traitor."

Diegen was sitting casually in his ivory chair, cleaning his nails with a sharp knife. He looked bored though his features were brooding. Graffias quickly and silently left the room and reappeared within moments, dragging a bedraggled and pathetic-looking creature behind him.

With pointed ears, sharp features, and long limbs, the creature, Hamir, looked very much like an elf. His skin had a slight, translucent blue sheen to it, his eyes were lilac with sapphire blue pupils, and his platinum blonde hair cascaded to the middle of his back like an unmoving waterfall of locks.

It was clear he had been tortured for quite some time and it was expected that all the fight had been beaten out of his spirit. Diegen was sorely mistaken in this last assumption and was, for once, taken by surprise by the creature being dropped to the cold floor in front of his chair.

"He refuses to talk further, my Lord."

"Very well, Graffias, get the cloak." As Graffias left the room yet again, Diegen studied Hamir. "You're pathetic," he practically spat. "If you tell me what you know, I will spare your life. This is your last chance."

"You've killed my family and have stripped me of all decency. What more do I have to live for? You're a monster and I hope you are found by justice one day and rot in Hell," replied Hamir.

Diegen appeared to be unmoved by the accusations and harsh words of his prisoner. Instead, he sat back in his chair and began to pick his nails with his knife once more.

"If it's a painful death you wish for, wish granted," was his response.

Just then, Graffias entered the room with a sort of cloak made chain mail clutched in his gloved hands. "Stand, Hamir," ordered Diegen, but Hamir only looked at him with tired eyes.

"It seems I'll have to help you then, Hamir." And with those words, the elf-like creature screamed in agonizing pain, shooting up into the most erect standing position—clearly having nothing to do with his own volition. The evil Cantelian ruler's eyes were set ablaze with blue-fired irises and he let out a cruel laugh.

"I warned you but you are too foolish. This is what happens when you dare to cross me by becoming a spy. Your death will serve as a warning to those who think they can get away with disloyalty. Graffias, the cloak!"

Diegen's top mercenary did as commanded, without even the blink of an eye. He threw the metal cloak on top of Hamir and worse screams poured out of the creature's mouth. If he even articulated words, they were so filled with pain and anguish that nothing he said could possibly be deciphered. Once the cloak was completely covering his frame, sizzling sounds and smells of burning flesh filled the air. Slowly, the metal lowered in height as poor Hamir melted and evaporated to death.

Within minutes, he was no more and steamy, blue vapors emanated from the blanket of chain mail sprawled on the floor. After another minute, the vapors ceased and Diegen got up from his chair. He snapped his fingers and the incense sticks placed in holders on the walls were lit, pouring forth a rich, cinnamon scent.

"Put the cloak away. It has served its purpose for today."

Without a word, Graffias obeyed and gathered the cloak, careful to avoid any exposed flesh on his body. Then he left the room for the third time that day. Not even a speck of dust remained at the site of Hamir's death. Diegen strode over to use the magic of the Vaskur, inhaling deeply the scent of the incense now filling the room. The blue liquid stirred and a half rat, half man face was looking out of the surface.

"Kumani," Diegen started. "Do you have the

girl?" Kumani nodded back, giving a few squeaks to indicate the positive answer to the question.

"Good. You know what to do. The girl should give us leverage and cause enough chaos to prevent the other tribes from working together with your idiot of an uncle. Remember, if you fulfill your duties, your curse and your father's will be lifted. If you fail me, I will personally pay you a visit and you will wish you had never said yes to me in the first place. Do you understand?" Kumani nodded his head vigorously.

"Begin to set the plan in to motion. I will contact you later this evening. Do NOT fail me." And with that final warning, the blue liquid in the Vaskur became murky and the rat man's face dissolved, only to change to another face—a black, furry, and red-eyed face.

"Vang, those ignorant tribes people are headed to the beach. Be ready for them and kill them all. Every last one of them. I am tired of waiting for them to cease their rebellion. If you ever want to see your human form again, you will do what it takes to be successful. Do you understand?"

"Yes, Lord Diegen."

"Very good. Report back to me as soon as you have the situation under control." The Vaskur once again became murky and Vang's face was no longer visible in the blue liquid. Instead, the basin's contents were still and non-reflective. Diegen strutted arrogantly to his chair, seated himself, and looked pleased for the first time in days.

Akeen was miserable. He was certain that Kodu would have executed him and was puzzled why his life had been spared. Of course he knew that the foreign teenagers had *something* to do with his temporary situation and wondered whom they were and why the chief chose to listen to them instead of his brother.

Though he felt such gratitude to have at least another day to live, he almost wished that the sentence had been more permanent; he was so distraught over losing Resina. Every night, he dreamed of her and would wake up feeling so helpless that he failed to find her. Being lost in thought distracted Akeen from hearing the door of the hut open slowly. He finally looked up when he sensed a presence. Standing before him was a cloaked figure.

"Who are you?" Akeen asked.

Answering back in the tribal tongue, a man's voice said, "I am Goden and I am here to release you from this prison to go back to your people. There isn't much time...we must hurry." He bent down to help Akeen untie the crude ropes around his wrists and ankles and helped him stand.

"Will not the guards stop us?" he asked his rescuer.

"No, I have taken care of them. Quickly now, we

must get to the edge of the village and I will tell you what you need to know before you go back to your father."

As Goden helped Akeen hobble out the door of the hut, the young warrior noticed two things: the guards appeared to be unconscious on the ground and the more Goden touched him, the better he felt. By the time they reached a thicker part of the jungle, he could walk normally once again. He wanted to ask Goden about it, but was interrupted.

"Akeen, listen carefully. I know you have many questions for me, but that must wait until another time. You must go to your father and tell him to gather the warriors of your tribe, find Kodu's people, and fight with them as allies, tonight. If you can get the tribes to work together, you will be able to save Resina and the young foreigner, Keira. This *must* be done tonight or all hope of seeing the woman you love alive will be lost. Go now. Help will come soon, but do all you can in your power to follow my instructions. Go!"

Akeen knew his way back to his tribe's village easily. Though he had been a hunter and fighter for most of his young life, he had never run as fast as he did that night. He reached the village in less than twenty minutes and shouted at the top of his lungs to wake up everyone.

Once the shock of his return died down, he quickly explained all that Goden had shared with him. After much deliberation, Akeen's father decided to call on their wise man, Nazoo.

"I have had a vision; we should do as the boy says. This Goden he speaks of...he is the Great Spirit and one the Brotherhood told us about. He will lead the Chosen Ones to defeat the Dark One. Tonight is the only chance we have to save our people and our island." With that, all the villagers gathered their weapons and set off in the direction of the beach.

It was probably past midnight. As soon as Kodu stepped forward into the open, a group of yellow eyes came nearer. My suspicions had been correct: the eyes belonged to the cat tribe but they were all in human form. And unless my eyes were deceiving me, I could have sworn that Akeen stood next to the man who looked like a chief.

How the heck did he get to be out here and look so...recovered? Kodu noticed him as well and opened his eyes as wide as they would go. This was getting intense. The other chief spoke first but we couldn't understand anything he was saying. Kodu replied and they went back and forth for a bit.

Then, both chiefs walked back to their people, still mostly hidden by the night and the jungle. Cantelia not only had two suns, but two moons as well. The evening was not as dark as Earth's, making it a little easier to see all that transpired.

When Kodu reached us, he motioned for all to stand. Cautiously, all the tribes people rose from the ground, holding their spears and other weapons pointed at the ground. Even *I* knew this meant that some sort of peace pact was in place—for how long, who could say. Either way, I felt encouraged. Wasn't this exactly what Goden wanted us to accomplish?

Before we could become cozy, however, loud yells thundered through the jungle and stampeding feet made the ground tremble. We braced ourselves for the worst. What more could go wrong?

We definitely did not have time for this. I felt more annoyance at the interruption than fear. From our right, close to where we had been captured the prior day, a group of warriors slowed down their pace and silenced their yells. Though their spears were initially in an attacking position, slightly raised above their heads, the men lowered them as soon as they came within twenty feet of Kodu and Feldor's tribes.

This had to have been the boar tribe—the tribe of Wata, if I remembered Kodu correctly. I supposed that the one in the group of warriors with the most intricate headdress on had to be Wata—and my supposition was correct.

Only he, Wata, stepped forward, palms raised in a surrender gesture. *Well, this just continues to get more and more interesting.* He said something I couldn't understand, but Kodu and Feldor met him in the middle. Moments later, they all laughed heartily, clasping each other's forearms. Kodu turned back to his tribe after that, sprinting toward us. I envied the fact that he was barely out of breath.

He eyed each one of us and said, "We fight tonight with Feldor and Wata. Wata wise man say he have dream to fight with us. We fight and win, we fight and die. We fight to end."

Daniel spoke up. "Chief, we're not very skilled, but we're with you. We will do what we can to end this curse. I think that's why we've been brought here to your island. It's time." Then Daniel looked at the rest of us. "Right, guys?" He raised an eyebrow and gave a stern look.

"Yep, we're in," Ben responded for the group. "Let's go." Even if we wanted to protest, what would the use have been? I could sense that everything having to do with the fate of the islanders and us would be culminated according to the events that transpired from the night. Oh boy.

Now that the tribes were united, this abnormal mix of calm and complete terror ran through my body. I wondered if Goden would show up, but maybe we had to do this—all of this—on our own, just like everything else. If we were unsuccessful in our attempts, the curse would still loom over the island and we'd be stuck on this crazy planet for yet another day—or more.

That thought alone helped me to internally cowgirl up, as my grandfather would have told me to do, and I marched forward with everyone, determination as my middle name.

Upon reaching full-on beach, I realized that we were nearing the same spot where everything had begun—the stone table of sorts, stained with old fruit and animal blood, a putrescent odor reaching my nose in waves. I tried not to think about how much it made me want to vomit right then and there, choosing instead to walk more swiftly. Right when our large group passed the table, low and threatening growls erupted ahead of us. I shivered.

All around us, tribesmen took a hunting stance, completely coming to a standstill. Those in front crept forward quietly, getting a sense for what waited ahead. Then I saw them—those red, gleaming eyes, coming closer and closer. The jaguars were headed for us, a hungry look in those red eyes. The came in shiny black waves of blue-black fur, their heavy paws thundering over the sand.

Some even rose out of the water, with droplets glistening in the light of the two moons. It was one of the creepiest sights I'd ever laid my eyes on. The warriors all did some kind of high-pitched battle cry and everyone charged forward. I stayed close to the tail end of the procession with Heather.

Just as Geoffrey had pointed out the day before, I didn't know how to fight and now was not a good time to try my lack of skills on this one. Nonetheless, I kept the rough spear I had tight in my right hand, feeling splinters beginning to break skin. I didn't care though;

the spear could very well have been the tool to save my life. I'd take a splinter or two for that reassurance any day.

There were probably fifty to sixty of the large, black, and sleek jaguars. Since they were about as large as Clydesdale horses, it was hard to not feel overpowered. We had about three hundred, but the jaguars had strength and weight on their side. Thankfully, these tribesmen were clever. I mean, they were hunters for goodness sake! Of *course* they could figure out how to kill any animal. Right?

When the din of battle began, casualties happened instantaneously. I counted three jaguars go down, but couldn't tell how many warriors were severely injured or dead. My stomach was in knots. It continued like this for a few minutes. One or two of the beasts were struck down or sustained serious injuries, but a handful of warriors went down for each jaguar. The ratio strength-wise sucked, to say the least.

Our situation was becoming desperate. This was not at all what I had in mind, especially since I had been trying to follow everything Goden had shared with me. And again, I asked myself, *Where the heck is he!* While thinking about Goden, someone or something practically flew by Heather and me with inhuman speed. But when he slowed down, I could tell that he was human. Maybe.

Not too long after, four more sped past us: two men and two women. They wore a type of leather material, resembling armor, and carried large swords. Who knew exactly *who* they were, but it appeared they were on our side. Skillfully, each stranger slashed at beast after beast, helping the tribes to gain some optimism and rally their strength. Though Heather and I were still waiting in the back of the fighting lines, mostly protected by the clump of warriors in front of us, one of the jaguars found an opening and began to gallop towards us.

"Alex! One of those things is coming at us!" Heather shrieked. She grabbed my arm tightly and for a few seconds, my first reaction was one of panic. But my adrenaline kick-started my survival instincts.

I grabbed my arm back from Heather and said, "Heather, this is no time to panic; we need to fight. Throw your spear when I tell you to or we'll be someone's dinner." Reluctantly, she followed my example and got in a fighting stance. I had never done anything like this before, but time was running out. I couldn't think; I just had to act.

When the jaguar came bouncing closer to us, maybe about twenty-five feet away, I yelled, "Now, Heather!" and we both threw our spears fast and hard. Heather's barely scraped the black furred creature, only causing it agitation. However, mine pierced it right between the eyes—a lucky shot, I guessed—and stopped it dead in its tracks. Literally. Before we could celebrate, though, another jaguar took its place, hunger for death glowing in its eyes. We had no more weapons on us—a very dismal outlook.

Suddenly, a woman jumped over Heather and me—yes, jumped *over*—and landed easily, right in between us and the gruesome beast. She held a spiked club in her right hand and a crude whip in the other. While cracking the whip in the air, she launched herself straight for the jaguar, yelling something loud and foreign. It caught the jaguar by surprise, stopping it from coming closer. Unfortunately for the animal, it was no match for this warrior woman, and without further warning, she crushed in its skull with her club. Whoa.

She turned to us and yelled in perfect English, "Girls, go up to that cave and release the two young women. I have killed the beasts guarding it, and have tied up the traitors. I will follow as soon as I can, but must help the tribes first. Go, quickly!"

We immediately obeyed and ran fast. Something silver glistened in the moonlight; it was a knife and I picked it up along the way, just in case. Something familiar hung about the air of that place and then it struck me—this was the exact same cave where I had met Goden.

We entered from a different side than the night I had been there, but nonetheless, that was it all right. Two jaguars lay dead at the mouth of the cave and Heather and I stepped over them cautiously.

"Hello?" I asked, voice trembling. "Anyone here? Keira?" I thought I heard slight moans ahead and ventured further to investigate, knife drawn. Heather stayed close behind. It was hard to see everything, but there were torches along the walls that gave off some light. I nearly tripped myself by running into something—something soft. I bent down and felt someone. "Keira?!" The voice that answered wasn't Keira's. It belonged to a young woman.

"Resina," she said in a pained voice. She *was* alive! I felt so relieved but knew we still had to find Keira.

"Alex?" asked a shaky voice. "Alex, is that you?"

"Yes, Keira. Where are you?" I crawled past Resina and found Keira within a few feet. "Are you okay? Did they hurt you?"

She said everything so quickly I could barely understand anything. "I think I'm okay. They only hurt me a little bit but nothing serious. They just tied me up tight and kinda left me here. It was awful, Alex. I'm so glad you found me. I didn't know if they were going to come back and kill me or something." Then she began to sob uncontrollably.

"It's okay now, I've got you. Shh. We need to concentrate and get out of here. Can you walk if I untie you?"

"I think so," she said tearfully.

"Heather, untie Resina and take her outside but be careful, okay? I'm gonna help Keira." The cave was just barely beginning to become lighter. It must have been close to sunrise, which meant that the tribes would soon change back to their animal forms. I could see a little better and used the faint light to find where I needed to cut Keira's ropes. Suddenly, Keira's eyes became wide with alarm.

"What is it," I questioned.

"Spi...spid...spiders!" Keira pointed upward. I followed the direction with my eyes and became horrified. The ceiling was teeming with rainbow-colored spiders. The torches were dimming and some spiders were beginning to lower themselves. They were dangerously close—perhaps only fifteen feet above us.

"Okay, let's get out of here," I whispered. The ropes were pretty tight, so I sawed away with urgency. Keira was nearly in hysterics as she watched more spiders begin to drop from the ceiling. Some were swinging on their silky web strings, waiting for the torches to completely burn out. They knew snacks were waiting for them below. I tried not to think about it and kept hacking away at the stubborn ropes. "Keira, you really need to hold still and shut up so I can get us both out of here alive." Thankfully, she momentarily calmed.

Finally, her limbs broke free. One of the torches went out, just ten feet away from us. A handful of spiders lowered completely, and scampered toward us while making loud popping and cracking noises.

"Run, Keira!"

I grabbed her gruffly by the arm and we ran to the opening of the cave, the spiders still after us. Now that there was more light, I noticed something Heather and I failed to recognize when we entered: out cold, Falu and Kumani were tied up against one of the cave walls.

"Keira, run to the beach and I'll be right there!"

Conviction and compassion took over in the moment of danger. I *had* to rescue Falu and Kumani, even though they were our enemies. Spiders were still headed for the mouth of the cave and one by one, torches were dying out. Without thinking, I grabbed the torch closest to the opening. It still had some of its "juice". I threw it on the droves of spiders crawling toward Falu and Kumani and they instantly went up in flames. Those that didn't burn scattered away, but others that were further away from the fire were marching like an insect army. There was no more time.

I grabbed Kumani first and dragged him out of the cave as quickly as I could. Then I went back in for Falu. He was heavier and harder to drag out. A spider was just starting to crawl on one of his legs, but I kicked it off. My heart was racing and the last reserves of adrenaline I had pumped into full force.

With a heavy grunt, I pulled Falu quickly from the cave and down the lumpy path. Too bad if he got scrapes and cuts from the small rocks; he had made his choice. He was lucky I chose to save his life. Heather yelled something when we reached the sand.

"Alex! There's a spider on your back! Don't move!"

Feast Island

I dropped Falu with a loud thud to the ground and was paralyzed. There were still spiders running toward us down the path. How was I going to escape this time?

Without warning, I felt something swish past my back. I risked looking to the side where a spear landed with a heavy clunk. The spider that had been ready to attack me was speared through like a shish kabob, rainbow guts spewing out of its wound. Even out in the open, the bad smell made my stomach churn.

My savior was the same warrior woman who had told us to go to the cave initially. She not only carried an extra spear, but had a curved sword in a sheath attached to a belt around her waist. In her left hand, she had a brightly lit torch. She approached the spiders that were coming closer and stopped abruptly. Then, she spit liquid out of her mouth, right onto the flames of the torch. Whatever it was, the liquid was flammable and flames landed on the army of spiders, completely incinerating them. Hallelujah. She threw the torch on the smoky pile and walked toward me.

"You are very brave," she began. I could feel myself blush. "I admire your courage. Take the young women down to the beach, away from here. I will take care of these traitors."

"Are you going to kill them?" I couldn't stop myself from asking. She looked amused and rolled her eyes.

"Unfortunately, Goden commanded that I spare

their lives. Had he said nothing, well..." she left it at that.

"Thank you," I replied. "For saving my life, that is. I thought I was done." She gave a small smile.

"You're welcome. Go, now. The others will meet you soon." As if she could read my mind, she added, "They are all safe. Go." I obeyed and walked to the girls. Heather was half supporting Resina and Keira was sitting on a large rock, crying.

"How...how...could...he?" she asked between sobs and heavy breathing.

"I don't know, Keira, but we really need to get out of here. I need to make sure you're okay. The best place to do that is out on the beach, away from the fighting and spiders, where there's more light. C'mon."

Heather, Resina, Keira, and I stayed well away from the stench of the bloody battle. I looked over Resina. Besides a few bruises and scrapes, she seemed to be okay—just in shock and hungry. Keira obviously fared better than her co-prisoner, but acted like she had been in captivity for months. I tried to be as patient as I could because I knew she had been traumatized. Keeping my mouth closed was a hard task, but I was successful; at least, this one time. The battle seemed to have dissipated and my deepest hope at that point was that the boys were all alive and well.

Thankfully, the four of them were walking slowly along the beach in our direction. I stood up to flag them down. Ben smiled wearily and did a little sprint to get to us before the others.

"Keira! Are you okay?"

"Yeah, I'm okay Ben. It was so awful though-" Thankfully, Keira was interrupted by the arrival of rest of the boys.

"Hey, girl," Daniel said, a little out of breath. "Glad to see you're all in one piece. The battle's over. There were some casualties on our side, but I think all the jaguars are dead—thank goodness."

"Yeah, if it wasn't for the Brotherhood showing up like that-" Justin started to say.

"Wait a minute," I interjected. "Those fierce warriors who joined in later are part of the Brotherhood?? No way!"

"Yes way," said Geoffrey, a little sarcasm in his tone. "I've never seen anyone fight as good as them— even on TV. They were pretty hardcore. And they came just in time. Justin here almost got sliced but one of the Brotherhood dudes stepped in and saved his a...er, butt."

"So where did they go?" Heather asked.

"Um...," Ben looked around, the light on the beach growing brighter. "I guess they left already. We did get to speak with them a bit though. They said that thanks to us getting the tribes to work together, the old magic on the island is stronger than the evil guy's. The curse is broken and the tribes people are free to live their lives as they did before this mess even happened. Kinda cool, huh?"

"Are you guys all okay?" I inquired.

"Yeah, yeah, we're fine. Just a few scrapes. Tell you what though, I can't wait to get a quick bite, wash off all this sand and blood, and get some sleep. I wish we didn't have to walk so far back. You need help Keira?" Daniel reached down to help her up and she gladly accepted. Ben reached down to help Heather, and I was surprised to get a hand from Geoffrey. Perhaps miracles still did happen.

We waited until the tribes people came to where we stood. Akeen was in the front of their procession, a downcast look on his face. But as he came closer and saw Resina with us, his countenance completely changed for the better and he ran to her, pulled her up from the ground, kissing her over and over. It was a sweet reunion. Watching them made me tear up. I felt a hand touch my shoulder lightly while I rubbed my eyes.

"Thank you." It was Kodu. "You save my Resina. I thank you, Chosen Ones. Our curse broken— we animals no more. Tomorrow we feast and honor you." I turned around and surprised the chief by taking his hand.

"Chief, it was our pleasure. Just remember that Goden was the one who told me what to do. None of us would be here without him." I smiled and he semi-smiled back at me. Squeezing my hand and then releasing it, he headed in the direction of his daughter and Akeen.

Feast Island

We began the long trek back to the village as both suns had just appeared on the horizon. I walked next to Ben.

"You know Alex, sometimes you sure have a temper, but you have your cool moments too. I really admire your courage. Most girls would have freaked but you seemed to be calm when there was a lot thrown our way today."

There were warm fuzzies dancing around in my body, but before they took over to make me stupid and giddy, I articulated a clear response of gratitude.

"Ben, that's one of the nicest things anyone has ever said to me. Thank you; it means a lot. You *always* seem calm, cool, and collected and I admire that. Thanks for sticking up for me." We looked each other in the eyes, smiled, and continued walking in tired silence until we reached our huts to wash up and sleep.

Chapter Sixteen: The Guardians

The next evening, Akeen and Resina were married. Their ceremony was simple enough and I'm sure anyone could feel the sense of camaraderie that now enveloped all the tribes. Though the occasion was a happy one, there were still those who had bittersweet feelings—the ones who had lost loved ones from the battle. Nevertheless, because of the unity of the three tribes, joy was the most prominent emotion for the night.

Food was abundant; everyone brought something to share and I thought my stomach would explode. We had been treated like kings and queens that evening and were even made honorary members of each tribe. The seven of us sat in a circle near a small fire, too full and tired to talk. Keira had nothing to say for once. But the silence felt comfortable. That is, until we spotted Kumani heading our way.

"What's *he* doing here?" she asked loudly, clearly not caring that he was in hearing range.

She crossed her arms and turned the opposite direction, away from him. Still, he continued to come closer to our group and for once, I actually had interest in what he could possibly have to say to Keira or any of the rest of us. He approached our group without his usual, arrogant strut. Instead, he actually looked humble and miserable. He stopped at the edge of our circle and looked down at Keira. She scooted away and he had a pained look on his face.

"I know you do not wish to speak to me or want to hear what I have to say, but I will say it anyway. I can only say that I am sorry, though you will not believe me. If I must face punishment soon from the evil one, I will gladly take it if I know it will bring you a feeling of justice. I do not or could not ever deserve your forgiveness." He knelt down and spoke softly, "But I will dare to ask for it." He waited for a bit until Keira turned around to face him.

"Go away," she replied tersely. She stood up, walked over to Daniel, and crouched behind him—almost as protection. Daniel, though amused, played his role as protector and glared at Kumani.

"I think it's best if you listen to her," he said fiercely. Kumani didn't even react; he simply got up and walked away. Maybe he truly was sorry. Was I going soft?

"I can't *believe* he had the *nerve* to ask for me to forgive him! How could I *ever* get over something like a kidnapping!"

Keira was absolutely flustered and she had a right to be so. I probably would have shared her exact sentiments if I were in her shoes. I watched Kumani shuffle towards the jungle, disappearing into the thick foliage. I did feel for the guy a bit. Around lunchtime, Daniel had overheard Kodu saying that Falu was nowhere to be found. Either he had fled the island or was permanently punished by the Evil One. Whatever happened, Kumani lost his father, and no matter how evil Falu was, he was still Kumani's dad. My heart, for whatever reason, went out to him.

Moments later, someone else emerged from the same spot: Goden. I rubbed my eyes, trying to see if I had been hallucinating. But no, there he appeared, just as real as in my dreams. Maybe that was it! Maybe I was in a dream state and that was why I could see him. The only bummer thing was that the others wouldn't be able to see him. When he finally reached our group, he spoke to me.

"Well done, Alexandra. You have succeeded in bringing the tribes together, helping them to break the tragic curse placed upon them."

"Thank you, sir...uh, Goden. Am I dreaming again?" I asked.

"Wait a minute," interrupted Heather. "*This* is Goden?!"

"What! You can *see* him? You can *actually see him*?" I was astonished.

"Yes, silly. Did you think you were dreaming again?" Ben stood up and strode past me, right to Goden. "Sir," he began, "sorry we had a hard time believing everything you told Alex. I'm sure we screwed stuff up a lot. But thank you for warning us about what you could. I just don't understand why you didn't tell us everything."

Goden smiled at him and put his hand on Ben's shoulder. "Ben, sometimes it's best to leave things to be discovered. If I told you everything, you would never have learned to trust Alexandra like you did. You may have been over confident too. Sometimes it is more dangerous than knowing every little detail. No, simply knowing enough is usually best. I was close all the time too, just in case."

"Then why didn't you come sooner?" asked Keira, a little angrily. "You could have prevented my kidnapping!"

"I know you cannot understand now, but sometimes horrible situations can bring about good. I will say no more on the subject, Keira, because your heart is not ready to receive it. However, I will tell you that I was always near, making sure your life was protected." Keira only frowned at his words and crossed her arms. It wasn't her best look.

"Goden, are you staying for a while?" I asked.

"For a little while, yes. Then I must get all of you home."

"Oh, great! Thank you! I can't wait to get a real shower, and eat carbs, and...," Heather looked sheepish. "And see my mom." Goden smiled at that.

"Soon enough, Heather. Soon enough. Do you

mind if I join you?"

"Please, sit down, sir." Daniel motioned to an empty mat next to his spot and Goden took it. I could hardly contain the pleasure I felt, knowing that my new friends could see and hear him too.

"Do you all remember what the name of this planet, Cantelia, means?" he asked us.

"Yes, 'Land of Song'," answered Justin.

"That is correct, Justin. Have any of you noticed that no music has been played—even for the wedding feast?"

"Yeah, actually, I did," I responded. I thought it was strange at first but never pondered it further. "Is that significant, Goden?"

"Yes, it is. Lord Diegen, as he is called by many, has forbidden any kind of music to be played or listened to. Without music, the heart of this planet and its people is dying. That is why you must all work together and be careful who you trust when you are here." He looked at each one of us in the eye.

"But I thought you said we'd be going home?" queried Geoffrey.

"You will be tonight, but I am referring to the future," said Goden.

"We're coming back again?" Justin was probably the only one excited to hear this. Goden chuckled and answered him.

"Correct, Justin. There is more to be done and believe it or not, you are all part of the solution to ridding this place of darkness. I will be watching you and the Brotherhood will help you as they can. This planet needs you more than you know."

"But, what can we do? We're just a bunch of freshman in high school!" Ben blurted all this out, a puzzled look on his face.

"I cannot say all you want to hear, but I can tell you this: Diegen wants to not only destroy this planet, but yours as well. There is something special in each one of you—something that scares him and something that could very well save two worlds. But enough of that for now. Quickly, come with me.

I wondered if Goden somehow "cloaked" us from the tribes; no one seemed to take notice that we were leaving. We didn't speak much to one another. I think everyone was tired from all the festivities. Plus, none of us had any idea as to the method of our return journey. The way felt familiar and once we arrived at the beach, I could see why. We were right in front of the spider-infested cave. I shuddered and closed my eyes. Goden began leading us up to the cave. The boys followed, but the girls and I stopped. Ben noticed and turned around.

"What's wrong?" he asked. I didn't answer his question because I had a question of my own for Goden.

"Goden? Are you seriously taking us through there to get home? What about the spiders?"

"Trust me," was his reply.

"Goden, I trust you and all, but I don't trust those spiders. If only you'd seen what happened last night-"

But he cut me off there and said more sternly, "Trust me." Then he turned around and marched toward the cave again. The boys continued with him and the girls and I hesitated. I let out a heavy sigh.

"Well, if we don't want to live in the jungle, I guess we have to do what he says and trust him. Come on, guys. Let's go before anything else weird pops out and tried to eat us."

The three of us ran to catch up with the rest of our party and we entered the dark cave, completely terrified. I found Geoffrey and walked close to him. I must have caught him in a tender moment, because patted my shoulder and whispered, "It'll be okay, Alex." That was all I needed to bite the bullet and walk deeper into the cave.

Surprisingly, nothing attacked us. We got to the very back of the cave and right when I thought, *Now how is he going to get us through solid rock?*, a beam of light grew from the cave wall. It opened to an archway and Goden stepped through. We followed him, of course, and went through the brightness.

At first, I was blinded by pure white, and I held fast to Geoffrey's arm. Then, the brightness decreased and once my eyes adjusted, I saw that we were in another cave. This one had gems that sparkled their own light—gems that I'd never seen in any jewelry store. Any celebrity would have killed to have any one of them as engagement rings or flashy jewelry for a red carpet premiere. I was in complete awe.

We walked further and some glowing figures approached us. I grabbed Geoffrey's arm even tighter and went forward with caution. Goden smiled and held his hand up at them.

"Greetings," he said. Only one spoke in return.

"Goden, thank you for your help in protecting the portal. I'm afraid we will only be able to hold the Dark Lord off a few more times. He has become stronger and once he finds us..." He ended there.

"But enough of that. You have a task for us, yes? We need to take the Chosen Ones home?"

"Yes," Goden replied. "They must return—for now." Then he turned to us. "The Spirits of the lake will take you home, young ones. I will see you again."

He walked back to the brightened archway of the cave, went through, and sealed it. We were left with ghostly, light, spirit people-things. You know, the typical caretakers of any teenagers trying to get home from another planet. Right.

"This way, children," the Spirit told us. He (I think it was a he) led us past more bejeweled caverns and finally to one with a pool of dark water. There were canoes lined up at the rocky shore and man, dressed in old-fashioned Native American garb, was standing by them. When the Spirit said the man's name, we all jumped.

"Star of Day, take these children home." The man nodded and motioned for us to get into the canoes. Daniel, Justin, and Ben took one. Next, Keira, Geoffrey, and Heather took another. I shared one with the legendary warrior himself. Out of all the things that had happened to us, this was the most surreal. I couldn't believe it was all true. Talk about getting up close and personal with your research topic.

"This way," he said simply. He paddled the canoe expertly and the others followed us. There seemed to be a small opening and we were headed for it.

"So," I began to question, "are you *really* the guardian of Spirit Lake?"

"Yes."

"Oh," was all I could think of as a response.

My brain seemed to be numb and I couldn't think of anything interesting to say. It was probably best to keep quiet anyway. We were closer to the light and just as with Goden, the nearer we got, the brighter it became. When I thought it would blind me, everything became dark and I lost all feeling.

Chapter Seventeen: Project Due

Sand and dirt were mixed in with my saliva and I coughed up water. I was face down on the ground, wondering where I was. A hand touched my back.

"You okay, Alex?" Heather asked.

"Where are we?" I managed to speak.

"We're back home," Ben said. "Here, let me help you up. We're on the North Beach. The boat's here too. It looks okay, but my grandfather isn't going to be too happy."

"And more importantly, our cell phones work! I tried yours, by the way," Heather said. "It's still the same day we left; only an hour's passed. Really weird. Even Justin's camera equipment is in the boat and seems to be working just fine."

Slightly disoriented and sopping wet, I took Ben's hand and he pulled me up. The sun was just about to set and no one was around, except for the seven of us. Daniel offered to walk Heather and I to our bikes so we could get home, but we both said we'd be fine. Geoffrey left right away, but Keira opted to stay with Daniel, Justin and Ben, until her ride came.

Heather and I walked quickly to our bikes and went to our neighborhood together.

"Well…see you tomorrow?" Heather asked.

"Ya, I'll see you tomorrow. Be safe, okay?"

Fortunately, when I got to my house, no one was home. Grandma was out bowling, Mom was at work, Lauren was probably out with her boyfriend, and Sean left a note saying that went to meet some friends for pizza. I quickly showered, then headed straight for my room to finish the remainder of my biology homework. It was eight when I turned out the lights. My dreams were filled with the images of the battle that took place between the tribes and the jaguars. Red eyes glistening in the dark, hungry for my flesh, haunted me. Though my mind was awake, my body was dead tired and I had to stay trapped in my dreams until the alarm buzzed in my ear at six in the morning.

It was Friday; the day after we had successfully began a video shoot for our project. Sighing, I picked up a small stone and tried to make it skip a few times over the water only to make a large plop sound on my first attempt. I thought back to Goden's parting words: "We will all meet again—and soon." What did he mean by "soon"?

Releasing another sigh, I resorted to throwing rocks until a nearby fisherman gave me an evil look. I had arrived early to North Beach so I could reflect on all the crazy events that had taken place. Everyone came on time and we got through the last shots pretty easily. Thankfully, no whirlpool sucked us to a parallel universe, but I did think I saw something resembling the ghosts.

"Okay guys, that's a wrap!" Justin said cheerfully. "Let's go enjoy the weekend and we'll work on the paper and other stuff next week."

Two weeks went by faster than any amount of time I could remember. Our essay was stellar and our video presentation was even better. We totally aced the assignment and gave some impressive information about the legend of the lake—with a twist.

We told the story of what happened to us—in a way—and it was so fantastical that no one had any idea it was based on actual events. But the project and my grade in English was no longer my main concern. I had no more dreams about Cantelia. In fact, I stopped dreaming altogether. It was all very strange. Though I wasn't itching to go on another adventure again, I wanted so badly to speak with Goden and get some answers. I could only hope he'd speak to me in another dream or choose to bring us all back to Cantelia sooner rather than later. There was nothing I could do but talk to my new friends about it when no one else was around.

After we were finished with the project and school was out for the day, I went to the lake for the afternoon. There was something about being there that gave me a little more peace, strange as that was. I sat by the dam, watching the sun set slowly. Footsteps crunched the rocks into the dirt and sand. When I looked at the person approaching me, I realized it was Geoffrey.

"Hey," I said with a smile. "What are you doing here?"

"Well, actually, I felt this urge to come here but now that I'm here, I don't really know what to do."

"That's strange," was all I could think of as a response. Geoffrey only nodded. He surprised me by sitting down and scooting close. After a few minutes of silence, he practically exploded.

"Why us? I mean, why did any of this happen in the first place? Doesn't it bother you that we don't know more? Why didn't Goden give us more details? I don't know that I want to ever go back to that crazy place, but it seems we don't have a choice, do we?" He sounded a bit angry—more like the Geoffrey I was used to.

I let out a sigh. These were the exact questions I had been thinking about since our return and I didn't have answers for him. "I don't know, but I'm sure everyone who's ever been chosen for something uncertain asks themselves the same thing. Think about all the good we did for those tribes and the island. Doesn't it feel great to realize that we did something we though we were incapable of?"

"Maybe...I dunno. It's just plain crazy. If you guys didn't remember the same things that I do, I would have checked in to the mental institution. I didn't even believe in magic until two weeks ago."

"Yeah, I know what you mean. I guess we'll just have to wait and see what comes next." Again, Geoffrey nodded a silent agreement. We sat there without speaking until the sun was barely a sliver of light above the horizon. Before we left, I turned to look across the lake one more time. A transparent figure looked straight at me and waved. I waved back. Would nothing surprise me from now on?

Epilogue: Diegen's Disappointment

Diegen no longer sat in his tall white chair, calm and collected. Instead, he was pacing the floor of the circular room, throwing curses in between strides. The torches in the room were ablaze, just as much as his anger.

He still couldn't figure out why the Vaskur would not allow him to see the children—for now he knew the aliens who had been on the island were children—and that frustrated him to no end. It must have been due to the protection Goden had placed upon them, similar to why he couldn't kill Kumani.

Somehow, he knew this was only the beginning and had to figure out a way to put an end to Goden and his little "army". This had to stop and soon. The door opened just then, interrupting his angry and vindictive thoughts.

"My Lord, he is here."

"Bring in the failure, Graffias."

Graffias threw Falu down on the hard, cool, marble floor. He had already been tortured and was barely recognizable. "Lord Diegen," he began to say in his native tongue.

"Do not call me by my name; you are not worthy, you incompetent fool!" Diegen spit on Falu but Falu remained motionless on the ground. "You are a failure, Falu. I would have killed your son in front of you first, but that...that *Goden*," he made a twisted face, practically snarling, "has somehow protected him. But no matter. Someone has to pay for the casualties my army sustained and you will have to do. You should have stayed with your tribe. But since you were too coward to face them, you must face me."

"No! Please...my Lord...please have mercy! It was the Brotherhood and those children...the prophecy..." Falu protested. Diegen's face started to reshape itself.

"*What* did you say?" he sneered. "Do not *ever* mention that rubbish again! It is time for you to die painfully, fool!" His fingers became elongated and his pupils changed to black oil pools. Falu shrieked in pain, crying for mercy, but never receiving any.

"My eyes, my eyes! I can't see!"

"Yes, I know," Diegen said, lips curled in a smile. He then relinquished Falu's tortuous pain and looked at his favorite mercenary. "Graffias, bring in the box." As he commanded his mercenary, Diegen said something in a forgotten language and the torches dimmed greatly once he stopped speaking.

Graffias immediately obeyed and left the room

for mere seconds, returning with a wooden crate. He pried it open with his bare hands and threw the contents on Falu. Ten Kongulos were immediately attracted to the blood smell that hung about the man writhing in pain.

Popping and cracking sounds could be heard, echoing throughout the small chamber. Falu only made whimpering sounds at this point. Once the sharp teeth of the spiders were exposed, and their bodies were constricted like upside-down cones, they immediately retracted their ten, long legs and lowered their bodies.

Their sharp teeth bore into Falu's flesh like cavity drills and he screamed in excruciating pain, but no relief came. He began convulsing and finally: silence. The spiders left only bones. When they were completely finished with their meal, their teeth disappeared back into their bodies.

Diegen lifted one hand and made motions in the air. The spiders began to float off the ground, unable to move. They were placed back into the crate and Graffias had a mallet ready for shutting them in with no chance of escape. The bones of Falu sat on the cold, marble floor. Instantly, the torches resumed their initial glow and burned brightly once again. Diegen looked at Falu's remains and stood up, shaking invisible dust off his long robe.

"Graffias, clean this up." And with that, the evil ruler left the chamber to receive a royal visitor.

Spirit Lake and Cantelian Key

Places

Pollock Pines: A medium sized "town" with a small population in northern California, where Alex and her classmates reside.

Spirit Lake: The main lake in Pollock Pines. Legend says there are spirits who guide the lake, hiding some mysterious secret. Some residents and tourists have claimed to have seen ghost-like figures towards the evening.

Cantelia: A planet at the far edge of the Milky Way Galaxy, in the Taurus constellation. Cantelia means "Land of Song" and has two suns—binary stars. There is a portal on Cantelia that connects to Earth, guarded by spirits in their own dimension.

Sikuku: Island to which the teenagers are transported, also known as "Feast Island". Sikuku is one of the major lands in Cantelia, but populated sparsely, due to a curse rumored to have plagued the island for quite some time.

People

Alexandra Hill: The natural leader of her peer group in English class. She describes herself as nerdy and blunt, but with a compassionate side.

Benjamin Thompson: One of the cute guys in Alex's class. Currently dating Lydia Snippens. Ben is sweet, smart, and straightforward, and is close to his grandfather.

Daniel Kerry: Dan is very athletic and confident. He can be very practical and logical—except when angered.

Justin Kerry: Brother and fraternal twin of Daniel. Very shy and tends to stutter when nervous.

Keira Casanoda: Keira, half Japanese and half

Portuguese, is a striking beauty. She can be very rude and narcissistic, and is known as one of the cliché "mean girls" in her class.

Heather Riley: Originally from Los Angeles, Heather is tall, quirky, and clumsy. She reads books as often as Keira looks in the mirror—very often.

Geoffrey Mitchell: The bad boy of the freshman class, who happens to be the most attractive. It is rumored he's spent some time in Juvenile Hall.

Mrs. Brown: The freshman English teacher who holds a mysterious and ethereal air about her.

Diegen: The supreme ruler of Cantelia. He holds dangerous and mysterious powers, most of which have yet to be made known. He requires the people and beings of Cantelia to offer up flesh sacrifices twice in their calendar year.

Propus: Royal Advisor to Lord Diegen.

Graffias: Head mercenary for Lord Diegen; of the Kotka race.

Vang: Leader of the evil henchmen, all of whom are cursed to remain as jaguars until the tribes people completely surrender to Lord Diegen.

Kodu: Chief of the "rat tribe".

Falu: Brother to Kodu.

Kumani: Nephew to Kodu.

Feldor: Chief of the "cat tribe".

Akeen: Son of Feldor; engaged to Resina, daughter of Kodu.

Wata: Chief of the "boar tribe".

Goden: Spirit guide to the teenagers and leader to the Brotherhood. Has mysterious powers that even the Brotherhood don't understand.

Brotherhood: Group of twelve beings who are keepers of the Prophecy. Only eleven are currently residing in Cantelia.

Vocabulary

Vaskur: An enchanted basin that holds a liquid-like substance, giving those who use it the power to see anything and communicate with anyone on the planet of Cantelia. The Vaskur was once used as a means to protect the beings of the planet, but is now used as a means to their detriment.

Kotka: A race of Cantelians who are, by nature, mercenaries. They have distinct marks on their scalps: intricate designs and patterns of raised skin. Kotkas who are active mercenaries keep their heads shaved as a means of identification and pride. Those who have chosen to overcome their inherent nature grow their hair out. Since they look like human beings, they can easily blend in among many varied communities. To turn away from their natural life means death, if caught.

Kongulo: Very large, ten-legged, rainbow-colored spiders. Native only to Sikuku, extremely poisonous and carnivorous. They respond to loud noises by attacking, live in dark caves, and fear the heat of fire.

Here's a sneak peek at book two of the
Spirit Lake Series:
<u>The Wrong Fairytale</u>

I thought my legs were going to burn off. I had only been running for a few minutes, but it felt like hours had passed—long, painful hours. Looking quickly to my right, I could see that Justin was keeping pace with me. I had known he was there because he wasn't very good at keeping quiet, but I wanted to get a visual. It felt more real that way, I guess.

The buzzing sound continued to get louder, which most likely meant it was getting closer. Or rather, *they* were getting closer. All the debris on the forest floor threatened to make us stumble, or worse: fall and be annihilated. This wasn't how I imagined the end of my life.

About the Author

Tamar Hela was born and raised in the Bay Area of California, where she currently resides with her family. Since the age of ten, many of her teachers have encouraged her to pursue a career in writing fiction. Tamar has always had a knack for words, loving the art of storytelling. As a musician and artist, she understands the importance of captivating an audience through various mediums, but especially loves using words to create visual images for readers. When she's not writing, business planning, teaching, singing, having coffee with a good friend, or dreaming up some crazy scheme, she can be found curled up with a good book.

Feast Island is Tamar's first published work of fiction. She is a published poet and her poem, *Hope*, can be found in the anthology *Live Life: The Daydreamer's Journal*. Daydreaming is what prompted Tamar to start writing and she encourages those around her to dream big, all the time. For more information on Tamar, visit her website: www.tamarhela.com.

AUG 1 7 2012

Made in the USA
Charleston, SC
05 July 2012